STREET DREAMZ DISCLAIMER: This is a work of fiction and this statement is included to inform the reader that any celebrity name(s), business name(s), locations, and organizations that are stated in the content of this book are real. However, they are used in a way that is purely fictional.

JAZZY KITTY PUBLICATIONS
PRESENTS

Street
DREAMZ
Ery Thing Ain't Wht It Seems

JERZ TOSTON

Street Dreamz

Ery thing Ain't What It Seems

By: Jerz Toston

Cover Art Created By KREATIVEGRAFIKS.COM

Logo Designs By Andre M. Saunders

Editor: Anelda L. Attaway

© 2018 Jerz Toston

ISBN 978-0-6921060-2-0

Library of Congress Control Number: 2018941022

All rights reserved. This book is protected under the copyright laws of the United States of America. This book may not be copied or reprinted for commercial gain or profit. The use of short quotations or occasional page copying for personal or group study is permitted and encouraged. Permission will be granted upon request. For Worldwide Distribution, available in Paperback. Printed in the United States of America. Published by Jazzy Kitty Marketing & Publishing, LLC. Dba Jazzy Kitty Publications utilizing Microsoft Publishing Software. Please be advised this book has strong language and content. Parental Advisory is suggested due to mature content. Disclaimer: This is a work of fiction and that any celebrity name(s), business name, locations, products, and organizations while real are used in a way that is purely fictional.

ACKNOWLEDGMENTS

First, all praise and thanks to Allah (SWT) without Him none of this would be possible.

I want to tell my kids Kai, Meesh, Lil' Jerz, Deivyan, Riya, and Ceer; I love y'all until the death of me.

To my sisters Ericka, Felisha, and Nika. I LOVE Y'ALL.

To my bro Pounds, my folks on lockdown C-How, Matim, and Dae-Dae I got y'all until they FREE Y'ALL.

To my bros from the 8th Kill, Hov, Big Head, Crumb, Chulo, Dulla, Break, and Mr. Shafee himself, I didn't forget you this time lil' bro. (LOL)

My BF's Deb and Sissy. I LOVE Y'ALL.

Cool Shoes keep doing you lil' bro.

Mom Dukes, you said the sky is the limit, this is #3, love you Mommy.

My barber Craig for keeping a nigga sharp.

To Anelda and the staff at Jazzy Kitty Publications, thanks for believing in me and bringing my vision to life.

Lastly, but not least, my other half, my best friend and soul mate Tambra. I know I can be a handful at times, but you always have my back no matter what and vice versa. It has been a long, rough past 7 months, but you've helped me get through it.

DEDICATION

This book is dedicated to my Big Sis (The Late Rez Ericka Toston) whom I lost on July 22, 2017.

Also, Mom Betty, Moe-Good, Mase Murda, Lil' Howie, and anyone else that has left us. Continue to look down on me.

I LOVE Y'ALL!

TABLE OF CONTENTS

TABLE OF CONTENTS

INTRODUCTION

Cannon always considered himself an average guy who like anybody else in the game wanted the cars, ice, girls, money, and fame. He told himself once he reached a certain point you get out, but at what cost. And with the help of his girl Tessa's dad, Tayo he will reach heights that he never knew existed. But as we know, the game is never that easy, there's always someone willing to do anything to take your spot, even kill.

The question is will he make it out alive or just another Hood Legend? Cannon has to be careful because when chasing STREET DREAMZ, ERY THING AIN'T WHAT IT SEEMS.

CHAPTER 1

Cannon and Sanchez Discuss the Work

"Listen, you been talk'n that rah-rah Shit for too long. If you gon' ride on that nigga then jus do it."

"Nah, I got his Bitch Ass in due time."

Cannon looked at Sanchez and shook his head while thinking, *"This nigga is a straight pussy."*

"What's up Cannon, why you lookin' at me like that?"

"You a better man then me cause that nigga would have been on a T-shirt. Real Shit."

"Trust, he'll soon be on one, real soon." I didn't respond because I didn't believe him.

"You'll see Cannon, you'll see."

"I hope so cause this nigga making me look weak," I thought to myself.

"Heeeey Cannon."

"What up Tessa?"

"You."

"I know that's right."

"What's up for later tonight?"

"You know my number, hit my jack."

"Yup, I sure will," she said licking her lips.

"Tessa you sum thing else.

"That's why you love it." I definitely couldn't deny that.

"I'll call you later," she said walking away.

"You do that." I know he's watching so let me give him something to look at.

"Daaaamn," Sanchez said watching Tessa's Fat Ass shake like an earthquake as she walked.

"Damn, what Nigga?" Cannon asked while watching Tessa himself, "she's fat as a muthafucker."

"Sanchez, please don't disrespect me like that," I said in a serious tone, so he knew I wasn't playing.

"Damn Playboy it was that serious," he shot back with a grin, "thought you was jus hittin' it."

"I am, but she's my folk."

"Nigga if I didn't know any better I'd say you caught feelings."

"I can't front, I'm feelin her, shit we been fuckin for a year now."

"Well, you better wife her up before sum body else does cause she definitely a ride or die."

"Man, my dick game too good, she ain't going nowhere not to mention she likes tha ones a nigga be throwing her way."

"Oh, so you paying for that?"

"Nigga, what the Fuck I look like, I ain't you." We both started laughing.

"You damn right, I pay cause I ain't got time for tha other Shit."

"I feel you, but on a more serious note, I'm thinking about droppin tha number on this work."

"Why?"

"Cause tha plug bout to drop it on me."

"Well Bro, that's more profit for us."

"Nah Bro, we tryin to kill tha comp."

"We already doin that, we got tha best Caine around, hands down."

"I know that, but if we drop tha number who can compete wit us?"

"I feel what you sayin."

"Did you collect that bread from Lil' Dae-Dae yet?"

"Yeah, and I hit him wit another ½."

"OK."

"Ran Off on tha Plug Twice," was the sound coming out of the white Range Rover that stopped on the corner. King nodded his head, so I nodded back.

"Fake Ass Nigga, I'm going to slump his Bitch Ass," I thought to myself.

"Yo Cannon," I heard Sanchez calling me breaking me from my thoughts.

"What's up?"

"I think we might need to dead this Shit at tha head."

"Dead what?"

"King putting work out here."

"Bro that Shit ain't messing wit my paper, so I don't give two Shits bout it. King knew even though I got to that bag I wouldn't hesitate to put my murder game down."

"You should've slump that Nigga when you had tha chance." I thought back on the day when I spared King's life.

"Now, I'm gonna ask this question one time and one time only. Which one of you niggaz stole from me?" Nobody said Shit.

"Oh a'ight, I see y'all think this is a game." I put my .45 up to Stinks head and pulled the trigger. Roz jumped as brain matter got all over his face and shirt.

"Now, would you like to answer me now?"

"It was Stink."

"I knew you'd say that." I saw movement from the corner of my eye, so I swung and pointed my gun, "nigga get ya Bitch Ass over here next to this Muthafucka."

"Y-Y-Y-o-o-o man, I I I don't want no p-p-p-problems," King said stuttering.

"Sure, you do, cause you back here being nosey."

"Nah, I was comin to check on my Lil' Cuz, that's all."

"Well, ya Lil' Cuz got himself in a little situation."

"I told you it was Stink Cannon."

"How convenient Stink can't defend himself."

"Man he…"

"Shut tha Fuck up!" I yelled, cutting him off, "I jus wanna know why you would steal from me as much love as I shown you?"

"I told you."

"Nigga, I don't see no hearing aid, so I know you can hear. Matter fact, since you said it was Stink that stole from me, I'll let you two argue about it Hell."

Boom! Boom! Two shots to his head sung him a sweet lullaby. Then, I aimed my .45 at King next.

"Whoa, Whoa, I ain't got Shit to do wit that."

"Nah you don't, but I won't be ya trump card later down tha line."

"Man, Cannon you ain't gotta worry bout me sayin Shit bout this."

"I know I won't," I said cocking my Shit back.

King closed his eyes, preparing to meet the same fate as Roz and Stink.

When he didn't feel Shit, he opened one eye. I stood there with pistol in hand shaking my head.

"I guess today is your lucky day. Now, get ya Bitch Ass Outta Here!" King took off running.

I yelled, "Don't make me regret it!"

"You feel me Bro?" Sanchez said once again bringing me out of my daydream.

"Yeah, I feel you," I said having no idea what he was talking about.

As if reading my mind Sanchez said, "You have no clue what I was talkin bout."

He was Damn sure right!

CHAPTER 2

Cannon & Tessa Is in Love

"Damn Bitch what took you so long? A bitch has been standing here knocking for 20 minutes."

"Bitch it ain't been that long and I was washing my ass."

"Let me find out you got a hot date wit Mr. Cannon."

"A Bitch gotta have a date to wash her Ass now?" Ha! Ha! Ha! Claire was laughing so hard she started choking.

"It was not that funny."

"Give me a Dutch so I can roll this sour up."

"Look in tha drawer by tha fridge and do not use those swishers."

"Bitch tha way Cannon snapped tha last time we used his pack, I wouldn't dare."

"So, Tessa, what's up wit y'all two anyway?"

"Ain't nothing up, we kool."

"Did you tell him you love him yet?" I gave her that look like Bitch what you talking about.

"Bitch don't give me that look; we been friends since we were 5 so, I know you *(I let out a long sigh)* I don't think he's ready for a relationship, so I haven't told him."

"It's been a year and he's clearly feelin you too."

"I know that, but I don't know if it's as strong as my feelings."

"Tess, it's only one way to find out."

"I know and to be honest, I plan on telling him tonight."

"After or before he blows ya back out?"

"Bitch do it matter?"

"Yup, cause if you wait til after, he's gonna think it's tha sex that got you saying it."

"Damn, I didn't think about that, you right."

"Ain't I always?"

"No."

"Well, did you at least introduce him to your dad?"

"Nope."

"Why not?"

"He already has a plug."

"Yeah, and 9 outta 10 your dad is most likely supplying him."

"You're probably right."

"Again, ain't I always?" I hate to admit, but this Bitch is always right 90% of the time.

"I'm jus sayin, since you gonna be wifey after tonight might as well help tha hubby get a plug." As if 'On Cue' my phone started to ring. (Ring, Ring, Ring)

"Hello."

"Hey Baby girl."

"Oh, hey Dad."

"Damn, that's all I get? Oh, hey Dad?"

"Stop it Dad. How are you?"

"I'm good," Tayo said and then asked, "did AJ drop that off to you yesterday?"

"Yes and thank you."

"No need to thank me, I'll always make sure you straight."

"I know and that's why I love you so much."

"Tell Claire I said hello and I send my love her way also."

"How do you know she's here?"

"Because when is she not...you two or more like sista's than best friends."

My dad was right, and he always treated Claire as his own. I told her what he said.

"Heeeey Dad, love you back."

Rumor has it that he had killed her father for not stepping up and claiming Claire.

"Oh yeah, before I forget, don't you two make any plans for Saturday night. I'm taking y'all to dinner."

"OK, I wanted to talk to you about sum thing anyway, so I'll do it then."

"Un oh? Let me dust off my .357."

"Dad, it's not like that."

"A'ight cause I won't hesitate to." I thought back to what he did to Mike a few years back and a smile crept on my face.

"I love you Daddy and we'll see you on Saturday."

"8 sharp."

"Yes, Father," I said while pushing end on my phone, "he's taking us to dinner Saturday at 8."

"A'ight, I'll be here at 7:30; you know how he is."

"Don't I."

"Well, I gotta date myself, so I'll see you tomorrow."

"A date wit who?"

"Do you tell me bout your dates?"

"Yes."

"Well, that's only cause its wit Cannon." We both laughed at that.

As Claire was opening the door Cannon was about to put a key in.

"Hey Cannon."

"What up Claire Bear?" All I could do was smile cause that's what he calls me.

"Sanchez is waiting on you." I turned around to see Tessa smiling.

Before she could say anything I quickly said, "I see she finally gave you a key and stepped out tha door."

"What you smiling for?"

"That sneaky Bitch jus told me she had a date, but she never said it was wit Sanchez."

Cannon started laughing and then said, "Maybe she didn't want you to know."

"Maybe, but on a more serious note..."

"Uh Oh, what I done did now?"

"Nuffin, I jus wanted to talk to you for a sec, if that's a'ight wit you?"

"Sure Babe, I'm all ears," he said pulling his ears out.

I couldn't help but laugh; not many people got to see or even knew about the playful gentle side of Cannon.

"Nah, but seriously, I'm listening," he said.

I was a little nervous, but Fuck it, "Listen, we've been doin' this for a year now and I need to be honest."

"What is she about to say," I thought to myself.

"Cannon I love you."

Without thinking I said, "I love you too."

Once I said it, I knew I couldn't take it back, but I didn't want to anyway because I honestly did love Tessa. She put her arms around my neck and pushed her tongue in my mouth. Believe it or not, this is the first time in a year we actually kissed. I instantly picked her up and proceeded to carry her into the bedroom. Once there, I laid her gently on the bed.

"Why are you jus staring at me?"

"Cause you're beautiful."

And she was. I could see the Dominican in her Bronze skin tone. One couldn't front, Tessa was bad as Hell 5-6", bronze skin, wavy shoulder-length hair, and an Ass that will make Nicki Minaj jealous, but hers was real. By the time I was done, we were both exhausted and more in love.

"I love you Cannon."

"I love you to Tessa."

"So, does that mean I'm wifey now?"

"Truth be told, you been wifey."

"Is that right?"

"Yup."

"Well, you better let ya other Bitches know."

"If there were any I would."

"Boy please, I know you got other Bitches."

"If I did would I be staying tha night wit you almost every night."

"Damn, he did have a point."

"You can tell your other niggaz to fall back or take a dirt nap."

I could tell he meant every word, but since I didn't have any that wasn't a worry of mines. I knew that besides the fact that Cannon got at that bag, he also had bodies under his belt.

Casually I said, "Babe, I haven't been wit anybody else in over a year."

"That's what I like to hear," I said kissing her ready for another round of steamy love making.

CHAPTER 3

Control the Entire City

"What it do King?"

"I can call it Float, but I won't."

"I feel you."

"Where is Strap?"

"Making sure that new shipment is right."

"I think we need to take over ya boy Cannon's spots, so we can control tha entire city."

"In due time, that nigga living on borrowed time; Float trust me."

King can still remember that day Cannon killed his Lil' Cuz in front of him and was holding on to that.

Strap walked in saying, "What up wit y'all, why y'all look so serious?"

"Shit, talkin bout ya boy Cannon."

"That Fuckin Nigga ain't my boy; King is tha only reason he's still breathing. I'll be the one to put that dog out of his misery."

"Well, what you waitin on?"

"Imma take everything he got and then end his life."

"Well, let's get this party started."

"Soon real soon Fellas, I promise."

"So, was that shipment on point?"

"Yeah, 21 kilos of cocaine and 3 kilos of heroin."

"Was it that Riggy Raw?"

"And you know it. My man Juan never disappoints."

"Yeah, but he needs to bring that number down."

"Nah, for tha quality work we get that's a Damn good number."

"Well, then we need not step on it so much, so that Shit can at least compete wit that Shit Cannon got out of there."

"I'm inclined to agree wit you on that."

"Say no more, it's a done deal."

"Well, a'ight I gotta go pick up this new shorty to see what that pussy like."

"I heard that." King said giving Float a high five.

"I gotta go take Banita sum food. She has to eat at a certain time or tha baby starts going crazy. Ha! Ha! Ha!"

"That Shit ain't funny Strap; I'll be glad when she has him, this Shit be bustin me."

"Trust me, I know all about that Shit." *As I stood up to leave I had remembered the $500 that Pep gave me to give Strap,* "oh yeah, here," I said handling him the money and before he could ask I said, "Pep."

"Oh yeah, I did win that bet that tha Cavs would come back to win tha chip after being down 3-1. Might as well take Lee-Lee to tha mall wit this."

"Man, you spoiled tha Shit out of ya daughter Bro."

"Nigga, in a few months you'll be doin tha same Shit."

"Sure, ya right."

We walked outside, dapped each other, and went our separate ways with plans of linking up in a few hours to handle the shipment we just got in.

CHAPTER 4

Claire & Her Dad

"Hey is Dad on his way?"

"Yeah, he said he'll be here in 15-20 minutes."

I didn't know where he would be taking us, so I just dressed casual. I looked at Claire with her Peach Romper and matching Louboutin's, which accented 5-7" frame very well. Claire was also pretty with her chocolate skin, gray eyes, and a nice Ass like the tennis player Serena Williams. She was often asked if her eyes were real. Simply cause, how many chocolate girls do you know with gray eyes?

"Sis, you look real cute, I'm lovin tha Romper."

"Thanks Sis, you look nice also." I was rocking and Cranberry YSL dress with matching open-toe shoes.

"Here, light this before dad pulls up honking like a madman."

No soon as we finished and were spraying ourselves with my favorite love spell the honking started. (HONK! HONK! HONK!)

We quickly walked out the door where my dad was waiting in his White on White S550 blasting some Trap or Die 3. I had to laugh cause my dad loved him some Damn Jeezy.

"This his new CD ain't it."

"Yeah, this jam is Fire," he said turning down the volume, "by tha way, you ladies look nice; I feel underdressed."

My dad was rocking a pair of Polo sky blue Capris with a white V-Neck Polo T-shirt, and sky blue and white Polo tennis shoes.

"You are not you are not underdressed Dad."

We pulled up to the Bonefish Grill which was my favorite spot. Once we were seated and our waiter came, I wasted no time ordering my favorite Bombay with light ice and orange juice.

"Henny and Coke for me."

"And you miss?"

"Long Island please."

"I'll be back to take your orders when I bring ya drinks."

"I could be wrong, but sum one has tha look of one who's in love." I looked at Claire knowing damn well he was talking about me.

"Well, I wouldn't call it love; jus a very strong case of like," Claire said smiling.

"That wouldn't happen to be Sanchez, now would it?"

"It might be."

"After one date?"

"We actually been seeing one another for bout 5½ months."

"Ooooooh, you Sneaky Lil' Bitch."

"Watch your mouth!"

"Sorry Dad."

"I didn't tell you cause I didn't want you to clown me."

"Now why would I do that?"

"Cause you said Sanchez was a Clown."

"I was talkin about a funny kind of clown."

"Oh," I said while laughing.

"We could have double dated."

"So, that means you're seeing sum body too?"

"I have a man Daddy."

"A man?" Claire said surprised.

"Yes, a man."

"So, I guess my advice worked?"

"Bitch yes, and after I told him I loved him, he told me he loved me too."

"Bitch shut up."

"I guess I'm not sittin here."

"Sorry Dad," we both said in unison. The waiter came back with our drinks and took our orders.

"Well, I'm happy for the both of you, I jus hope I don't have to dispose of them."

"No, you don't Dad; that's what I wanted to talk to you about."

"I'm all ears."

"Cannon has a nice plug, but I know you can probably beat his number and I'm sure your work is much better."

"I see."

"Cannon has tha best work in tha city and he moves a lot of it."

"And how do you know this?"

"I see and hear; and no, he does not have drugs in my house or does he involve me."

"He better not! Does he roll wit that clown boy they call King?"

"No, he doesn't even like King. In fact, I heard he spared his life a few years ago. When he killed his cousin and his boy for stealing from him." My dad scrunched his face.

"What's wrong Dad?"

"I heard about that and even though I did not know him, I respected him for that."

"Why Dad?" Claire asked.

"Simple, if he didn't kill them, they would label him as weak and never respect him." We continued to talk while we ate catching up.

When we pulled back up to my house, my dad gave us a kiss along with a few ones as he calls it.

"Love you Dad."

"I love you too, and I'll call you in a few days to set up a meeting wit your boyfriend."

CHAPTER 5

I'll Take Ya Life!

"So, what's tha deal wit you and Claire Bear?"

"What do you mean?"

"Nigga, you know what I mean."

"We jus friends, but I do like her."

"That pussy got you sprung."

"Bro, I ain't even hit it yet."

"Huh?"

"You heard me, I ain't hit."

"Damn, not mister, I jus pay and keep it moving."

"I know right. She's one of tha good ones."

"I know that's why I didn't try to hit; she might jus be wifey soon."

"Oh yeah, you definitely feeling her talkin like that."

"At least I can admit that."

"Well, so can I."

"Really?"

"Yup, Tessa is wifey; we made it official a few days ago."

"Damn, how that come about?"

"She told me she loved me, and I told her I felt the same way."

"Daaaamn, so you said tha big 3 words, huh?"

"Yup, and I meant 'em."

"We gotta double date. Ha! Ha! Ha!"

"Listen to you."

"Hey, this could be tha start of sum thing new for me Bro."

"I'm proud of you cause all that sleeping wit this chick and that chick, will catch up wit you."

"Nah, I use these," said Sanchez pulling out some Magnums.

"I thought you was going raw Dog."

"Hell nah, Bro, I might be a lot of things, but stupid ain't one."

"I know that's right."

"You Fucking wit that game tanite."

"Nah, I got Shit to do."

"Claire Bear?"

"Nah, some Shit I need to handle." I didn't ask what cause 9 outta 10, it was with a Bitch."

"A'ight, I'll hit you later, I'm bout to get at Los."

"You need me to come wit you?"

"Nah, I got it you hold down tha fort."

"I always do Bro."

Before stepping off I said, "I see traffic done picked up over there."

"Yeah, but it ain't stoppin nuffin over here though."

"Guess ol' boy finally stop bookin that Shit up."

"Guess so."

"A'ight I'll hit you, soon as I handle this."

Two hours later, I was about to go handle what I needed to take care of since the sun had finally set.

"Aye yo Duck."

"What up Sanchez?"

"You gonna be a'ight out here?"

"Of course," he said exposing his Glock that was tucked in his waistline.

"Kool, I gotta make a run, be back in bout an hour."

"No problem, handle ya biz."

"I ain't going nowhere, it's money to be made."

30 minutes later, I was pulling up a few blocks from my destination. I got out and looked around to make sure nobody saw me and then proceeded to walk up the street. I saw who I was looking for standing with two other guys. They were the only three out, which was good. Pulling my hoodie tight, I casually walked up on the 3 of them.

"Yo my Man, what you need Coke or Heroin?"

"I'll take ya life!!!" (POP! POP! POP! POP!) My four shots hit their intended targets.

"Hold on Poppi," said Miguel backing up.

I took my hood off just enough so only he could see my face. The look in his eyes said it all.

"Did you think I would let you get away wit that?"

"Do you know who I am and what will happen if you kill me?"

"Yup, and I could care less."

I pointed my pistol in his face and pulled the trigger. He was dead instantly. While standing over top of him, I emptied the remaining bullets in his face.

"Let your family grieve, you Bitch!"

I pulled my hoodie back down and then walked off. Since this was a block that frequently heard gunshots, I knew the police wouldn't come for a while, but when they did they would have work to do tonight.

CHAPTER 6

No Man Will Ever Take His Place

"Hey Babe."

"What up Baby girl? You look tired."

"Yeah, it's been a long, exhausting day."

"Wanna talk about it?"

"Not really."

"OK, no problem. Do you know this muthafucker Los had me come meet him jus to tell me he would be going up on tha number."

"Oh wow."

"Guest he does wanna talk about it," I thought to myself.

"He had me bring all that Fuckin paper jus to say that. Tha muthafucker should've jus told me to meet somewhere so we could Fuckin talk."

"Well, why didn't he bring tha work?"

"Cause he didn't know if I would wanna Fuck wit tha new number. He knows I don't really have a choice, ery body else has trash." I just listened, waiting for him to finish.

"But the muthafucker jus told me that he would be droppin tha number. That's not it, then he says he's about to do biz wit Kings Bitch Ass. I should slump both their Bitch Asses."

Now it was my turn to speak, "Baby, if you don't mind me ask'n, how much is he try'n to charge you now?"

"30."

"Racks?" I asked shocked.

"Yeah, I was kool wit tha 26, but Damn, that's a whole four Racks?"

"Listen, I might be able to help you out Babe." He looked at me as if I just called his mom a Slut!

"Ha! Ha! Ha! No disrespect Baby girl, but how can you help me out in this situation?"

"I know sum body that has weight."

"I've never involved you in my biz, so you don't know, but Baby I deal wit major weight not no 8 balls or zips."

"I mean I kinda figured that, you don't strike me as no 8 ball or zip Ass Nigga. Plus, my folk has unlimited amount of it, not to mention, it'll make Los work seem like some stepped on Shit."

"I don't worry about that Babe."

"I do and I'm sure tha number is much lower than 30."

"At this day and time numbers are high, so I understand Los number, but I'm a loyal customer, so don't go up on me."

"I feel you, but it's obvious that Los doesn't have any loyalty cause if he did, he wouldn't jump tha price up that high and he definitely wouldn't deal wit tha competition."

"Maybe he jus wants more money."

"Baby, if he's really gettin at a bag, then it's not about no money...Trust me."

Listening to Tessa talk really made me love and respect her more; this was a side of her I've never seen. But it actually turned a nigga on.

"So, what tha deal wit your peeps? And I hope it's not an old boyfriend or a nigga that has tha hots for you."

I didn't respond, but as if on cue my phone started to sing, "He Brings Me Joy." I saw the look on Cannon's face which made me smile on the inside.

"Hello."

"Hey Daddy's Girl."

"Hey, I was jus talkin bout you to my man," I said so Cannon could relax, which he did.

"Oh, where are you?"

"Yes."

"Are you home now?"

"Yes."

"Fine, I'll be by in 20 minutes then."

"A'ight fine, we'll be here."

After hanging up with Cannon said, "So, I guess he's on his way?"

"Yup."

"That's a Hell of a ringtone you got for him." I still didn't respond, I just skipped the subject.

After about 25 minutes, there was a knock on the door. As soon as I opened the door my dad stepped in and gave me a hug and kiss and then as usual complimented me on how good I looked. I could see Cannon wanted to say something, but probably wanted to see what was up with the business at hand first. I was finding it kind of cute so I didn't say nothing yet.

"Cannon this is Tayo and Tayo, this is Cannon." My dad looked at me.

I quickly said, "Bizness." And he understood.

I filled my dad in on what Cannon had just explained to me and then I let them talk.

"I have a few questions if you don't mind me ask'n?"

"Depends on what they are," Cannon said standing his ground, which made my dad smile.

"I see, well, you jus answer tha ones you're comfortable wit."

"Fair enough."

"A'ight who's your supplier?"

"Los."

"Carlos Santiago?"

"Yes, you know him?"

"Very well, Carlos or Los as you call him, used to work for me." This caused Cannon to sit up.

"He worked for me up til about 5 years ago."

"What happened?"

"Simple, he got big headed."

"He's doing pretty good."

"You're his main income."

"He jus told me he's about to deal wit Bitch Ass King."

"I'm sure you're familiar wit tha term middle man."

"Huh?"

"It's very simple, you place your order, he calls tha Gomez family and they front him the kilos. Then he calls you, once he has them. Need I go on or do you understand?"

"I fully understand. Damn, I wonder how much they charge him?"

"21," said Tayo nonchalantly, "you're probably wondering how I know this? I know about all my competitors. My next question, how much was he charging you?"

"26 at first, but he jus informed me that tha number is now 30."

"Ha! Ha! Ha! Excuse me, I'm not laughing at you, but his greed. How many were you purchasing?"

"10 a week, sometimes 12.50."

"He's trying to profit 1000k off of you."

"What?" I could tell that Cannon was pissed.

"Yes, they jus dropped the price to 20 for him."

"He's Fuckin dead, Imma call his Bitch Ass for 10; kill him and take that Shit. Now, I'm not mad at the middleman, Shit that's the game I'm mad at his greed. They dropped the number on him, but you raised it on me. He thinks I'm a Fuckin Dummy. I'll show him."

"No need. Listen, I know you think what you had was tha best and you would, cause you have not had better…" I paused so he could absorb what I just said; "I have the best Coca in tha land."

"How much is 22?" I asked just to throw a price out there.

"Sure, if that's what you wanna give me," said Tayo with a big smile.

Tessa punched him in the arm. "Ouch!"

"That didn't hurt."

"Cannon, that is too much, if you grab 10 weekly like you say, I'll charge you old school prices."

"And what's that?"

"18k." Cannon eyes got extremely big.

"That's definitely old school, I've never seen them for less than 24."

"You've never dealt wit me. I'm pretty sure you would like to test it first to make sure it's what I say it is."

"Nah, I'll take your word for it."

"I rather you try it out first."

"No need."

"A'ight, jus let me know when you're ready."

"Since you're at 18k and I was payin 26, that gives me a lot more room to play."

"Indeed, it does. So, I'll take 14 right now, if you're ready."

"We can do it first thing in the morn, if it's not a problem for you?"

"Not at all."

"Tessa call me at 6 am."

"Listen, no disrespect, but I'd rather deal wit you and not involve my girl." This made Tayo smile.

"Also, whatever you two had in tha past is simply that, in tha past." Tayo laughed so hard it was pissing Cannon off.

"Tessa will always be my heart and no other man will ever come between that, no man."

When Tessa didn't say anything, it pissed me off. Sensing that Cannon was about to explode I decided to defuse the situation.

"Cannon, he's right. No man will ever take his place, he will always be my first love."

"Hold up, am I hearing her right," I thought to myself.

"So, why did you tell me you love me jus to see if I would say it back?"

"No. I do love you."

"Cannon, I see we both share the same feelings for her which makes me happy."

"Listen, I'm not into sharing my woman. I love you Tessa, but not enough to share you. I also understand if you no longer want to do bizness."

"Listen, Cannon all I ask is that you treat her wit respect and never ever involve my daughter in your bizness."

"Hold up, did you say daughter?"

"Yes, Latessa is my only child, well my only biological child. Claire is also my daughter."

"This is your dad?"

"Yup, the one and only."

"I feel so stupid," I said putting my head down, "why didn't y'all say anything?"

"Wanted to see how you really felt about her and I have no doubt you love my Tessa."

"Wow."

"I'll have a phone for you in tha morn to only use when you want to call me."

"OK no problem."

"Welcome to a whole new playing field Cannon," Tayo said extending his hand.

"Happy to be a part of a real winning team."

"Talk to you guys in tha morning; 6 am Tessa."

"I know OK Dad." He gave me a kiss and then left.

"How you going to play me like that Baby girl?"

"I didn't play you, jus testing you."

"You almost got your pop hit."

"Yeah, a'ight Nigga, you would've had to hit me too."

"I could never do that to my Baby girl," I said kissing her forehead.

"Babe I'm starving."

"Me too."

"It's only 9 o'clock, let's slide to T.G.I. Fridays."

"If you drive," he said tossing me the keys.

CHAPTER 7

Damn Snake Ass Greedy Bastard

"You know I'm ready I'm really feeling you Claire."

"Now you got a Bitch blushing all crazy."

"Nah, I'm jus being real."

"I'm feelin you too Sanchez."

"Y'all good?"

"Let me get another Henny and Coke please."

"Anything for you miss?"

"I'll take another Long Island, and can you have them make it stronger?"

"Sure."

"Thank you."

"No problem."

"Damn."

"Damn what?"

"Stronger? That's your third one."

"Yeah, and tha last two were weak; I should be grooving by now."

"Hey y'all."

"Hey Tess, hey Cannon."

"What up Bro, y'all might as well join us, we jus ordered our food."

"We going to sit here wit them if it's a'ight."

"Sure, no problem." (The waiter hands them a menu)

"We don't need those, we know what we want."

"Kool, works for me."

I slid and besides Sanchez while Tessa slid by Claire Bear. The waiter came back with their drinks and was surprised to see us.

"Can I get you two sum thing to drink?"

"Yes, and you can take our orders as well."

After taking out orders, he asked if we wanted everything to come out together.

"It doesn't matter, whatever is easier for you."

"I'll be right back wit your drinks."

"Kool, make 'em strong please."

"I'll let tha bartender know."

"Good look Fam."

"Look you two, y'all been gettin real close lately."

"Claire bout to be my wifey," said Sanchez confidently.

"Oh, is that right?" Cannon asked.

Claire didn't say Shit, but she didn't have to cause her big ass Kool-Aid smile said it all.

"Well, you know you have to leave all ya Bitches Alone."

"Come on Tessa."

"Come on Tessa? What you not gonna have my sista out here looking dumb or fighting."

"I would never do that. Plus, I only had Fuck Buddies."

"Whatever you call it."

"Besides, not that it's any of your biz, but I haven't had none. It's damn near 6 months."

"Boy save that Shit."

"I haven't." Even Cannon had to look at him.

"Look, Cannon don't even believe you."

"Nah, I believe him cause he told me. I'm jus surprised he told y'all that." We continued to talk while we ate our food.

"DTB we don't trust Bitches."

"What up Lil' Dae-Dae?"

"Oh Shit! Word Damn! Sum body beat me to it! Lucky Mutha Fucker!"

"A'ight, I'll be back around in a lil bit."

"That was Lil' Dae-Dae, he said Tex and Miquel got killed on 27th and Tatnall."

"Oh Shit! Damn! Wow!" Was all we could say.

I looked at Sanchez try'n to see if he could give me any indication if he had made the call on it. I know he didn't do it, he wasn't built like that, so I thought anyway. When we finished Sanchez paid the bill and I handled the tip.

"You on ya way back to tha block?"

"Yeah, did you get wit Los?"

"Fuck Los, he's lucky I don't kill his Bitch Ass."

"Huh? Sanchez said clearly confused and very puzzled." I gave him the quick version of the story.

"Damn Snake Ass Greedy Bastard!"

"Fuck we gon do now?"

"Eat Nigga, you know I ain't goin out like that."

"So, you gon pay that high ass number he wants?"

"Fuck no! I wish I would, Tessa hook me up."

"Tessa?"

"Yeah Nigga, her pop, that nigga."

"Tessa, Tessa?"

"Yeah, wifey and Los use to work for him, but he got greedy."

"Damn, and he still alive?"

"No thanks to Los father, Tayo owed his father a favor."

"Oh, so his pop used it to save his son?"

"Bingo."

"What he gon charge, 22?"

"Nah, 18k."

"Get tha Fuck Outta Here."

"Seriously, and he assures me it'll make Los work seem like it was stepped on."

"Daaaaaamn, he got that straight from Colombia Shit!" (Honk! Honk!)

"I'll holla you in the morn, she wants some of this good loving."

"Lucky her, Ha! Ha! Ha!"

CHAPTER 8

The Meeting

At 6 am on the nose, Tessa was calling her dad. She wrote down and address on a piece of paper and then hung up. When I came out the bathroom she handed me the paper and let me know he was waiting on me. I stopped to grab the money, then 15 minutes later I was pulling up to the address Tessa had given me. I left the money in the car just in case something went down. Soon as I stepped on the porch the front door came open.

"Come in."

"Let me grab tha paper out of my car."

Tayo had to admit Cannon reminded him of himself, which was a good thing. After grabbing the money, I made my way inside the house which looked nothing like the outside.

"AJ this is Tessa's boyfriend Cannon."

"Cannon this is my right-hand AJ." We shook hands all the while I still had the duffle bag over my shoulder.

"Your money is safe in here."

"Oh, my bag, that's out of habit."

"Trust me I know, but anyway I wanted to show you a kilo of what you're getting and also cook one."

"Mr. Tayo, I trust you."

"I know you do, but I'm still going to show you."

As soon as he cut it open you could see the scales as well as smell it. So, I knew that was 100% raw.

"This is so pure you can put a ½ on it and it will still be tha best cut."

"I'd rather keep it tha way it is simply cause I know that it will move at a rapid pace."

"I don't need to make a mill off of one bird, I'm good wit 36k."

"This is why I like you Cannon, you're not greedy but smart."

"So that leaves me to believe that you will be selling your ounces at a rack."

"Yeah, everybody else is doing 1200."

"Smart very smart."

"But I'll let tha whole thing fly for 25k, if they get 30 or more I'll drop to 23k." I caught Tayo looking at AJ nodding his approval.

"Why would you do that wit this quality of work? Especially, when they can turn two into five?"

"Simple, I'm about tha quick-flip, if I spend 252k and bring back 322k that's a 70k profit."

"I'm kool wit that cause that's selling them at 23k, but I know that I'll make more than that." I saw Tayo smile as I was breaking down the math and my logic.

AJ cut in... "Aren't you afraid that sum body will get jealous or mad and come for you?"

"That's a very strong possibility, but know this, I will not hesitate to let my gun sing."

"There may be a time you're caught wit out it like now."

"You ever heard that saying about American Express AJ?"

"No."

"Never leave home wit out it," I said lifting up my shirt to reveal my .45 in my waistline.

Tayo looked at AJ and shook his head.

"Well, I'm glad he didn't want to blow our heads off and rob us."

"Nah, I'm not into that; I work hard for mines."

"Where will you keep this?"

"I have an apartment jus for this."

"Do you do your own cooking?"

"No doubt, that way I know what it is."

"Well, help yourself everything you need is already in tha kitchen." When I saw the big Pyrex pot I was like a kid at Christmas.

"Where did you get this? I've searched high and low for one like this. With the one I got I only can cook nine at a time."

I dropped the whole chicken in the pot and worked my magic. Within a few minutes I brought that chicken to life.

"Now that's what I'm talking about," I said more to myself and then I set it on the napkins.

"It looks like you know what you're doing."

"Mr. Tayo, when it comes to this, I'm the best."

"I know he lost out on it," Tayo thought to himself.

AJ set the scale next to it and turned it on.

"Be my guest," Cannon said moving so AJ could put it on the scale.

1,084 is what it read. Cannon smiled knowing he just proved Tayo's thought wrong.

"I must admit, I'm impressed. I surely thought you lost by the way you cooked it."

"I know you did; not too many people know how or about that dry cooking."

"I jus don't like my shit all weight then muthafuckers complain about how they lost out letting it dry out."

"This way no one complains and tha smokers get all oils wit no bake."

"This is 257k."

"That's too much."

"No, tha extra five is to show my gratitude and appreciation."

"Well, let's jus say you got that for five cause I was giving you that, so you could have extra money to take my Tessa out shopping."

"No disrespect Mr. Tayo, but I have more money; I'm not going all-in, not yet anyway."

"Don't worry Cannon, none taken, and you'll never need to go all in, this is tha start of sum thing beautiful; I promise."

"And I promise to make you a lot more money."

"I'm pretty confident you will." He motioned for AJ to get the duffle bag that was in the corner.

"Take this phone, only use it to contact me."

"Kool, but take this number because I won't have this phone on me but if I see your number I'll call back from that phone."

"OK, no problem." I walked out the door and the sun was starting to come up.

"I think he's the one AJ."

"Yeah Bro, you might be right."

CHAPTER 9

Nigga Where Is My Fuckin Spread

"Nigga, where is my Fuckin spread Nigga?" Strap was bagging up.

"What's funny?"

"You jus said Nigga twice in tha same sentence."

"Cut the bullshit Strap! Now where is my money?"

"I need a few more days." (SMACK)

"Nigga, you said that last week." (SMACK! SMACK! POP! POP!)

"Damn Nigga, now I'm not gon get my money."

"King, you wasn't getting that shit anyway."

"Yeah, you right. You talk to Float?"

"Nah, not since yesterday."

"I know you heard about Miguel, Tex, and Squash."

"Nah, who they body now?"

"Nobody, they got bodied."

"Word? Oh Shit! They must have been slippin, especially if all three of them got bodied."

"Yeah, I thought it might have been his work, but he ain't pick up when I hit him."

"Damn, let's get out of here."

15 minutes later, we pulled up on 24th and Carter to find Float talking shit as usual.

"What up y'all?"

"Damn, you can't pick up tha phone."

"Man, I left that shit over shorty's crib and she claiming it ain't there. I got a whole new phone."

"Why you ain't hit us?"

"Nigga, I don't know no numbers, only names."

"That ain't good. If sum thing happened, how you going to get in touch?"

"I don't know; good question."

"Was that your work last night?"

"Huh?"

"Miguel and his crew."

"Nah, what tha Fuck happened to them Clowns?"

"They all got bodied."

"Say word?"

"Word."

"Damn, who beat me to it?"

"Evidently sum one who wanted them more than you."

"Fuck! Fuck! Fuck!" Float yelled causing everyone to look. What he said to the ones that were still looking.

"Calm down Nigga."

I knew Float was pissed; he wanted Miguel bad. All the plans I had for that went back down the drain.

"Shit, I might as well go to his funeral and give him tha whole clip."

"Ha! Ha! Ha!"

"I'm dead serious Strap."

"I'm laughing cause I know you're serious as a fuckin heart attack. Man, Fuck 'em Float it's done."

"Yeah, guess you right; must have been their time," he says with a wicked grin, "anyway, what it looking like out here?"

"Money UAlready."

"Right, I'm bout to go thru a few spots, grab some spread from a few niggaz."

"I'm a stay out here wit Float," Strap said while tucking his pistol in his waist.

"Kool, I'll hit you later on this evening."

"A'ight, be safe."

"UAlready."

CHAPTER 10

I Need to Know Who Did This to My Son

"I need to know who did this to my son," Amelia Gomez with tear stained eyes.

"I'm already on it Mom," Cinco her middle son said.

Trans who was the oldest said, "I told him not to play tha front line, I told him."

Trans was trying to be strong for his mother, but you could clearly hear the pain in his voice when he spoke.

"There are a few different people he had beef wit."

"Well, let's snatch them up."

"Kool, but don't worry about Sanchez."

"Why not?"

"He's soft and doesn't have tha heart to do anything like this."

"Yeah, you're right about that."

"He's softer than ice cream on a hot summer day."

"Ha! Ha! Ha!" This causes Amelia to laugh.

"Listen, before we go grabbin people up, let me reach out to a few people to see what they know or can find out for me."

"You sure Mom?"

"Very, trust me on this son. We can't jus act on emotion and bring that kind of attention on us."

"No problem, we'll jus continue to conduct bizness as usual."

"Carlos said he might have another major player to add to tha mix."

"Good good."

"Los is starting to step it up."

"So, I've noticed. Did you drop his number like I told you?"

"Yup, did that two days ago."

"OK, so we should see an increase in his order."

"Hopefully."

"I have a few meetings, I'll talk to you boys later."

CHAPTER 11

He Passed All the Test

"So, how did tha meeting go wit Cannon's dad? And did he pass your test?"

"Ha! Ha! Ha! You think you know me."

"I do, and it wouldn't be you if you didn't put him through some kind of test."

"Yes, he did pass all tests."

"Damn, so how many did you throw at him?"

"It doesn't matter as long as he passed."

"Uncle AJ seems to really be impressed wit him."

"Wow, that says a lot cause Unc doesn't like anybody but you." (LOL)

"He loves you and Claire."

"You know what I mean."

"Tess, Cannon is very smart and trustworthy."

"I know."

"He definitely has a spot on my team, shit he has all the potential to run my organization."

"Wow! Hearing my dad say that really lets me know Cannon impressed them." As if on cue I heard Cannon's key going into the door.

"Well, I love you Dad and I'll call you tomorrow."

"OK love you too."

No soon as I pushed end, Cannon came walking in looking like he just won the Powerball.

"Hey Baby girl," he said while bending and planting a kiss on my forehead.

"I was about to call you to make sure you were safe."

"Oh yeah, I was handling biz after I left ya dad."

"How did that go?"

"Better than I could imagine."

"That's good, you looked like a different man."

"Baby, I feel like a different man. I'm bout ta Fuck this city of Wilmington up, they're not gonna know what hit 'em til it's too Fucking late."

"So, I take it your bizness wit Los is finished?"

"Tessa that shit was done when he jumped tha number four stacks."

"Did you let him know?"

"Fuck him! I ain't got ta tell him shit, he'll know when I don't call. Shit he can't even call me, I changed my number."

"Oh really?"

"Yeah, I texted it to you." I was about to say he didn't when I looked and saw that he did.

"I must have been on tha phone running my mouth when it came through."

"It's Friday, what do you say we had to King of Prussia and do a lil shoppin?"

"Hey, you know that's my favorite pastime."

"Let me call Claire and tell her there's a change of plans."

"I didn't mean to interfere wit y'all plans."

"Nah, we was jus going to Christiana Mall to get sum thing for tanite."

"What's going on tonight?"

"Doc B is having a party at tha Chase Center."

"You got tickets already?"

"The owner of Phat Cutz has them."

"Oh Craig?"

"I guess so."

"Damn, that's my barber, let me hit him to see if he got two more."

"Two?"

"Yeah, Sanchez might wanna go; let me hit him and see first."

After calling Sanchez and Craig I was on my way to get four tickets and then scoop him and Claire to hit King of Prussia.

"There's a parking spot right there Babe." I pulled in and cut the engine.

"I'll let you do ya thing," I said to Tessa as I was pulling out some money to give to her.

"No!" Sanchez yelled. We all looked at him.

"Bro, you plan on being here all day?"

"Nah."

"Well, you make that move and you will." Me and Claire laughed because he was damn sure right.

"I don't want to go wit them store for store."

"I feel you, but they'll be in tha same store as us, jus tha ladies' department." Cannon looked at me like what should I do.

"Babe he's right."

"Then let's go, we've wasted enough time."

Cannon reminded me of my dad wit this time shit, but I found it kinda cute. Our first stop was the Gucci store.

"If you find sum thing you like I'll be over here."

"A'ight."

"Tessa get whatever you like, it does not have to be jus for tanite."

"A'ight Babe."

"You too Claire."

"Oh OK," Claire said surprised.

"Bitch I was spending my own money."

"Well, now you're spending his."

"I'm not gonna go crazy cause you know a bitch can and will run a checkup."

"I know that's right," I said while high-fiving her.

"Damn Nigga, you must've finally tap that Ass."

"Nah, I'm jus showing her what being wit me is like." (LOL)

"I heard that Bro."

"Damn, these Gucci sneaks is it."

"Yeah, but you know you gotta put a shoe on for Doc B's parties."

"Yeah?"

"Yup, Cannon you got to get out more."

"I know."

"So how did it go this morning?"

"Let me jus say Los shit is trash compared to this."

"Word!" Sanchez said excitedly.

"Word and he had me cook a whole bird jus to show me what it was. Bro I didn't put shit on it and it came back $1,084."

"Stop playin."

"I'm dead tha Fuck serious."

"Before you say it, we not putting shit on it cause this is going ta ensure us all bizness once they get wind."

"I feel you."

"We're gonna let 'em fly for 25k, anything more than three we'll do 23k."

"Damn, you want tha whole city."

"Nah, jus 90% of it; gotta let a few others eat so won't be no bullshit."

"Definitely feel you on that Bro."

"We jus trying to dump quick and still profit at tha same time."

"Right."

"I already let my peoples know tha new number and tha work is 10x's better."

"Sanchez on tha breakdown for tha small guys 125, 250 and a stack."

"Kool, I'ma hit my peoples soon as we leave here."

It was three hours ago that we had stepped in the mall and the ladies were finally ready.

"Sorry Babe."

"It's kool, you good. Looks like you brought tha whole mall."

"It's been a while since I've been shoppin and I know I'm gonna be super busy in tha coming weeks."

"Right, so tonight we party hard."

"Yup, I'm going to Vanity Guard after Doc B's party."

"Well, I'm going wit you."

"Me too," Claire Bear said from the backseat.

"Doc's party is over at 1:30 am. I'll probably bounce by 12:15 to 12:30."

"I'm fine wit that."

"Guess I better bring my sneaks," said Sanchez.

"That's why I grabbed those Gucci sneakers too." We made it back to

Wilmington and no time.

"Claire be at my house by 9-9:30."

"A'ight, see you later."

"Sanchez don't forget to make those calls."

"Already on it Bro."

"Kool, I'm bout to handle some biz now to get this ball moving."

(The phone rings) *"He Brings Me Joy"*

"Hello Father."

"Hey is Cannon wit you?"

"Yes, we jus came from K.O.P."

"How long til you reach home?"

"In bout 3 minutes."

"A'ight, I'm out front waiting."

We pulled in my driveway and my dad got out wit a bag followed by my Uncle AJ.

"I've come bearing gifts," Tayo said laughing.

"Dad what did you buy me now?"

"Looks like you have enough things, but this isn't for you," he said handing the bag to Cannon.

Once we were inside Cannon looked in the bag and the biggest smile crossed his lips.

"My man," he said giving my dad dap and a hug.

"Damn what's in tha bag," I was wondering.

I tried to peek, but Cannon closed it and took it out to his car.

"What was that Dad?"

"What was what?" he asked playing dumb.

"In tha bag."

Before he could answer Cannon came in and said, "Don't worry about it." Tayo nodded letting Cannon know it was a good answer.

"Well a'ight, we got bizness to handle."

"So, you came to see Cannon?"

"Sum body seems upset," Uncle AJ said with a grin.

"No, I'm not and this is not y'all meeting spot." All three of them started laughing.

"Where was tha joke at?"

"Awe my Baby," my dad said hugging me which made me feel better.

"You're spoiled rotten," Uncle AJ said.

"I blame you two."

"We've created a monster AJ."

"Don't I know."

"Didn't you say y'all got bizness to handle?"

"I know you not putting us out?"

"I would never do such a thing to my dad and favorite uncle."

"We out AJ."

"Yeah Tayo, I know how to take a hint."

After my dad and uncle left I was ready to get me some. I walked up behind Cannon wrapping my arms around him.

"You are too spoiled."

"They did it," I said sliding my hand down to his private.

"Oooooh this is why you were rushing them out?"

"You better know it. I want you to bend me over the counter and Fuck tha dog Shit out of me." I turned around, so I was now facing her.

"Well."

"Well what?"

"What are you waiting for?"

"You're crazy."

"You think?" she said turning around and lifting her dress exposing her nakedness.

My Shit got rock hard.

"Are you going to get this pussy or what?" Tessa asked while leaning on the counter.

"Who am I to disappoint a lady in distress."

I let my pants fall to my ankles and then slid up on her. She bent over so I could just slide right up in her already moist box.

"Uuuumm," she said as soon as she felt the tip slide in.

I took my hand and rubbed my head against her clit causing her to let out a loud but soft moan.

"Oooooooh stop teasing me Daddy, I want to feel all 11 inches in me." I slowly slid inside her.

"Aaagghh Yes! Put it all tha way in me."

Once I was all the way in she screamed, "Now Fuck tha Shit out of this pussy!"

I started pounding the shit out of Tessa like it would be the last piece of pussy I ever got.

"Yeeeees Daddy Yeeeees! Like that! Get this pussy," she yelled while looking back at me only turning me on even more.

Tessa backed me up, so she was away from the counter. As I thrusted into her wit long hard strokes she bent down touching her toes while making her ass bounce.

"So, I see sum body was holding out on me," I said why matching her stroke for stroke.

"I couldn't give you everything, I had to save some of my tricks."

I went down and then came upward which caused her to yell out my name.

"Cannon! Oh Shit! Yeeees right there!" I continued to hit that spot until she exploded.

"Oooooh Fuck! Here it comes! Oooooh My God! I'm Cumming!!! Shit, Shit, Shit! Oh My God!"

I pulled out of her, she dropped down and got all of her juices and cum off me.

"There you go, all clean now let's finish."

Just as I set her on the counter my phone rang. *"You Can Count It Up It's All There"*

"I got to get this."

Tessa pulled me closer and then put me inside her gyrating her hips like a belly dancer.

"Yo."

"What it do Homie?"

"UAlready?"

"I'm waiting on you."

"A'ight, I'm in tha middle of sum thing. I'll be at you in about a half."

"Say no more, double my order."

"Got you, hit you when in route."

"Kool." I slid my phone on the counter and then picked Tessa up.

"That's right Daddy! Get your pussy!"And I was getting it too.

"I'm bout to Cum again Daddy!"

"Me too Baby, me too!"

10 seconds later, we were both Cumming at the same Damn time.

"Thanks Babe I needed that."

"No problem, anytime. Round two tonight so be ready."

"Great minds think alike," Tessa said while walking into the bathroom.

Damn my baby has tha softest sexiest body.

"Come wash up Baby."

"On my way now."

Once we were done I grabbed my phone and headed out the door.

"I'll be back by 9-9:30."

"I'll be ready."

CHAPTER 12

I Was Pleased with My New Deal

After meeting with Los I was pleased with my new deal; I would still deal with Juan on the heroin tip but Los on the Caine.

"So, how much is Los charging us?"

"27k."

"That's love compared to the 31k Juan was hittin us for."

"Yeah, and this that work Cannon be having."

"It's definitely a lot better so I have no doubt we will be taking over Cannon spots real soon."

"Willingly or forcefully?"

"I prefer forcefully," Strap said wit his Glock in his hand.

"Did you niggaz get ya lay for tonight?"

"Yeah," Float replied.

"Yeah, I grabbed sum thing yesterday from up top."

"Me too."

"You bringing out tha big boy tonight, I know."

"You better know it, I jus got her cleaned up."

"You tha only one in tha city wit that new Jag truck."

"Of course, I am," Kings said dapping both Float and Strap.

"I'm bout to go to tha crib and put some of this new work together."

"Ima be right here huggin tha block."

"Fuck it, I'll slide wit you, Float can hold this down by himself."

"Nah Nigga, I ain't never by myself, I always got my bitch wit me," he said exposing his nina.

"A'ight, hit us if you need us for anything."

"Sure will."

As we were pulling off I spotted something I've been trying to get with but haven't been successful. I pulled up next to her at that light and rolled down my window.

"Oh God let me act like I don't see or hear him," I said to myself.

I was trying to get her attention, but she was so into her radio that she didn't see me.

As soon as the light changed, I pressed down on the gas hoping he wouldn't follow me. Damn, I was happy when he turned the opposite way.

"Why you ain't jus hit tha horn?"

"No need, I'll catch her tanite."

CHAPTER 13

Vanity Grand

It was a little after 9 when Claire came strolling in looking like something off the Runway.

"Damn Sis you are killing that Roberto Cavalli dress."

I couldn't front Claire looked good and that cream and pink dress with her matching Jimmy Choo's. Her diamonds around her neck, wrists, and ears really set it off.

"I hope Sanchez got his leash," I said laughing.

"He doesn't need one, he knows who I'm going home wit."

"Right Sis right."

"You not even ready yet."

"Yes, I am, I jus need to put my shoes on."

Claire looked me up and down and then nodded her approval. I had a fat ass, but Tessa made my shit look small compared to hers.

"Bitch that all white is beautiful on you."

"Like my girl said, rock my all-white when I'm feeling Godly."

"Yeees Bitch Yeeees!"

All my All White Gucci Dress hugged every curve like it should but my cranberry, white and peach Gucci pumps set it off like Jada. I decided to put on my diamond name necklace and bracelet that my dad had gotten me last year for my birthday.

"Do these look right?" I asked as I was putting on my cranberry Gucci shades.

"Bitch of course wit that cranberry clutch."

"Here roll a few up, we in for a long night."

"I know we got to smoke this on tha way since we can't smoke in tha Chase."

"I know, but we can at Vanity."

We both looked at the door when we heard it being opened. My mouth dropped open when I saw Cannon walk through.

"Damn Baby you look good."

"Thanks, you must want me to catch a case tonight," he said staring me up and down.

"Did y'all plan this Claire?" asked pointing to both of us with the all-white.

"Nah, pure coincidental."

I had to admit we did look good together. Cannon had on a white Gucci Blazer and jeans wit a peach V-Neck and peach and white shoes. The Nigga was so icy I was cold just standing next to him. His diamond necklace with the cursive 'C' had so much ice in it that it was ridiculous. If that wasn't enough his watch, Oh My God, shit he even had diamond earrings. I wanted to rip his clothes off and suck him off right there where he stood.

"Get your mind out of tha gutter," Claire said snapping me out of my daze.

I just smiled.

"Where is this little Nigga at?" (Knock-Knock)

"Right here."

Cannon opened the door and then said, "My Bro clean up nice."

Sanchez came in looking like a new man. He was always on the block, so you would rarely catch him dressed with anything on but work clothes as he called it. So, to see him standing there with his cream linen Blazer and pants, pink V-Neck had me blown way. He also had his jewels on that was like Cannon but instead of the 'C' he wore a 'S'.

"Bitch y'all planned that," I said pointing to their clothes.

"Yup, we sure did."

We smoked 2 Dutches, took some pics and were out. By the time we arrived at the Chase it was 10 o'clock and the line was long as shit. I had to laugh when I saw King.

"Always wanna be the center of attention."

"I like his damn truck though," Cannon said.

"It's a'ight," Sanchez said.

"We don't hate bro, we give credit where credit is do."

"I know."

"Oh Shit! I forgot they didn't approve you for it when you tried to grab it, so you don't like 'em now."

"Fuck them trucks." We all started laughing.

"Shit I was tryin to build my credit up, I could've got my mom to get it in her name."

I pulled my S550 in Valet right behind Kings truck, but they had already gone inside.

"Nice ride," said the valet worker.

"Thanks." I rarely drove it, only on special events such as this.

"Damn, I don't feel like waiting in that long ass line." Sanchez looked at Claire like she lost her mind.

"We don't do long lines clearly you've been dealing wit tha wrong niggaz."

"Oh, excuse me."

We got in the VIP line and went straight in.

"Let's take a few pics and then hit the bar."

"Oh, shit tha real money in tha building shorty," the picture man said given us dap.

"Imma take 12 shorty and then I'll be back."

Once we were done Tessa put the pics in her clutch and said she had to use the ladies room.

"A'ight, will be in tha VIP, come on Claire walk wit me."

"I gotta go too."

"Fuck."

"What?" Before she could say shit, King was blocking her path.

"Damn, you look sexy as fuck." I didn't want to be rude, so I said thanks.

"That was me on tha side of you earlier at tha light."

"Oh yeah, I didn't see you," I said lying.

"I know you was too busy bumpin to your music."

"Ooooh, you saw that?"

"Yeah, but any way, what's up wit you?"

"I'm kool."

"Can I buy you a drink?"

"I'm here wit sum body and he might feel a certain way."

"Damn, bout a drink must be soft." At that point, I was ready to keep it moving.

"Excuse me, I gotta use tha bathroom."

"Damn Tessa, so you still FAT as ever."

"Don't disrespect me Strap."

"I wasn't, jus complimenting you. So whats up?"

"Boy please stop."

"You keep frontin."

"I'm not frontin I got a man."

"Oh yeah."

"Yeah."

"Who you wit?"

"It don't matter."

"You right, I'll get you."

"I doubt it," I said walking away.

"Girl they are so thirsty."

"Who you tellin, you would think by now they would know they ain't got a shot in Hell."

Two girls came in talking about King. I couldn't help but laugh as we walked out. We made our way to VIP but didn't see Cannon or Sanchez.

"Hey Sexy, you lookin for me?"

"Yup, I sure am," I said turning around looking into Sanchez eyes.

"What's wrong you OK?"

"Yeah, I jus need a drink."

"I got a bottle of Henny, but you probably want a Long Island."

"I'll drink some Henny tonight."

"Sum body is showing off."

"Hey there, he goes tha love of my life," Tessa said wrapping her arms around me.

"What's up Babe, I got us a bottle of Bombay."

"Good cause I could use a drink."

We all took down a few shots and then we were ready to get our party on. The DJ started to play that new Ace Boogie track My Shit and the place went crazy. While me and Tessa were dancing, I could see King and his flunkies staring at us and so could Tessa, so she gave them something to see. Just as the DJ switched to "She Got a Dunk" Tessa turned around throwing that ass all over me. I looked at Claire Bear who was doing the same thing to Sanchez.

"Yo look at those two clowns as niggaz," Strap said wit an obvious attitude, "I should go over and interrupt their dance."

"Nah, we'll get those Bitches." The same two girls that were in the bathroom walked up.

"Come on King, let me see if you can handle all this," she said pulling him to the floor.

The other girl followed her lead grabbing Strap. We were having a ball and a bitch was fucked up off the Bombay. The next thing we knew the lights came on because two Hoodrat Bitches were fighting over Float. The party was over now. I looked at my watch and it was only 12:19 which was kool since we were about to leave anyway.

"I guess they were going to let King and Strap hit it like they said in tha bedroom." Me and Claire started bagging up.

"What's so funny?"

"These chicken heads," I said and gave the valet my tix.

"Hope ya man don't wait up," Strap said to Claire.

"He doesn't have to, he's wit me," I kindly let him know while putting my arms around Cannon.

Cannon looked straight at Strap daring him to say something slick. Strap thought about it but decided not to. When the valet pulled up with my car everybody just stared.

"Yo Fam is that the new S550."

"Yeah."

"That Shit is nice."

King just looked, and thought *wait until my shit pulls up.* When it did, and nobody said shit, King got pissed. Cannon just smiled as he opened the door for Tessa. Even though his black on black Jag truck on 26's was nice, it couldn't compete with Cannon's cranberry on white S550 sitting on a pair of 22's.

"Cannon where y'all headed?" Lil' Dae-Dae asked.

"Vanity Grand."

"Hold up, me and my shorty gonna follow y'all; I'm parked right there," he said pointing to his cherry red 750 on 26's.

Seeing Lil' Dae-Dae's car made both Sanchez and Cannon smile. Cannon turned his volume up, *"If I Eat, My Whole Team Gonna Eat, One Shine We All Shine."*

He looked over at Strap and King gave them a head nod and slowly pulled off giving Lil' Dae-Dae enough time to get in his whip.

"What the fuck he's tryin to say?" King asked nobody in particular.

"Yeah, cause we all eatin over here," Strap said.

There was no doubt that they were making a few pennies, cause compared to what Cannon and his team were making that's exactly what they were making. It would only get worse once his new product touches the streets. Little did King know, Cannon had the same plans as he did shutting all his spots down.

"Let's go up Vanity and show this nigga how we do It."

King looked at Strap and nodded his agreement. The two ladies just hoped they were going too.

"You ladies wit us or you need to get dropped off?"

"Of course, we're wit you; tha night is still young."

"Strap do you need to grab some more spread or you good?"

"Nah, I'm good, I got 5 bands on me."

"Ard, me too."

"Sanchez, let's make some stripper happy tanite, this is our celebration on what's about to happen for us." Tessa smiled knowing she was the cause of it all.

"What you smiling bout?"

"I'm glad you and my dad hit it off."

"Why wouldn't we?" I stopped at one of our stash cribs to grab some more paper.

"Bro grab me 10."

"I got you."

"Matter fact, let me come in so I can piss."

"What y'all doing?" Lil' Dae-Dae asked.

"Grabbin some paper."

"Damn, do I got enough on me?" Lil' Dae-Dae wondered pulling out his mitten and counting it.

"Hold up Babe." Lil' Dae-Dae walked in.

"What's wrong?"

"Let me hold 5 bands, I'll give it back in tha morn unless y'all wanna stop by my stash crib?"

"Nah Lil' Bro you good, we were bringing you out this anyway," said

Sanchez passing him the 10 bands.

Before he could utter a word, Cannon said, "And we don't want it back; that's for you to have fun tanite cause after tanite Shit bout to get real for these niggaz."

"Oh Shit, Los must of dropped that number."

"Fuck Los, I cut him off. I got a real plug now and tha work 10x's better. So tonight, we celebrate, come on for they get restless."

Taylor was in my car talking to Tessa and Claire.

"Come on Babe."

CHAPTER 14

Make It Rain!

"I see is jumpin tonight, I hope we can still get a booth." We paid the 40 ones to park up front.

"I see ya boy came up," Sanchez said referring to King's truck that was also parked up front.

"That's only cause he heard you tell Lil' Dae-Dae this was where we was headed."

"Fuck that nigga, we here to celebrate and have fun." I saw a few people going in the side, so I figured those were the ones getting booths.

"What it do Big Man?"

"What up?"

"Think we can get a booth or are they gone?"

"Let me check, we might have one left."

He hit somebody on his walkie-talkie and 2 minutes later a White man in a suit appeared. The bouncer pointed to us and he walked over.

"Hello."

"What's up?"

"We have one booth left but it's going to cost 2500."

"No problem, we'll take it and 15,000 worth of ones to start out."

His eyes got big and then he said, "Well, since you doin it like that, jus give me two 2,000 for tha booth."

"Kool."

"I got it Big Bro," Lil' Dae-Dae said counting-out 2,000 from the money he had.

"Follow me, also your booth comes wit a bottle of Grey Goose and

Ciroc."

"We don't drink that."

"Um speak for yourself, I drink Ciroc."

"Oh, sorry Sis."

"You can substitute tha Goose."

"A'ight, give us any Henny."

"No problem."

"Plus, a bottle of Remy." Tessa cut me off before I could finish.

"I want my own bottle tonight Babe."

"No problem, also two bottles of Bombay. Claire Bear you want ya own also."

"Yeah, why not."

"Another bottle of Henny."

"A'ight that's another 1200." Lil' Dae-Dae paid for that too.

"Both of y'all give me 5 racks." And when they did, I handed it to the owner.

"That's 18,200."

"A'ight have them bring tha ones' wit tha bottles," he said extending his hand.

"No problem."

"Follow me."

He guided us to a booth that set up high away from the other booths. All eyes were on us as we made our way to the steps to our booth including King and Strap.

"Look at these Muthafucka's," said Strap as he made it rain causing tha strippers to go crazy.

A few minutes later, you could see the bottle girls headed our way with the sparklers indicating the bottles were about to be served. We definitely had all eyes as they came our way with 6 bottles of our drink and 3 trays with 5 stacks of money on each. The strippers saw it too as the DJ announced that it was about to go down. Between our ice and the ice that the girls had on we were definitely blinding the club. A few people thought we were new rappers, others thought we played ball. We balled just not for a team, in the league anyway. Lil' Dae-Dae and Tessa pulled out the sour and lit it up.

King thought to himself, *"Damn maybe I underestimated these niggaz cause they definitely jus threw away damn near 50 racks, he assumed anyway."*

While Strap was thinking, *"Maybe I should do a little homework and rob these bitch ass niggaz."*

For the first time Strap had to admit to himself that Cannon and his team was getting at that bag.

By 3:30 am we were all drunk and ready to go. As soon as the waitress brought our food we were out. Before we left the owner gave me a card with his name and number.

"Next time hit me in advance and I got you."

"No problem, I sure will." I gave King a head nod and walked out the door.

"Always a gentleman," Tessa said while laughing and holding on to me at the same time, "I wish y'all wasn't in tha car so I could give my baby some head all tha way home."

"Bitch you drunk."

"No Bitch I'm serious."

Sanchez said, "You wild."

"That's why he love me; ain't that right Baby?"

"Yup, sure is."

"Sanchez if you lucky my sis may pussy whip you tonight."

"Don't feed into it Baby," I said while massaging his already stiff meat.

As soon as we hit the door it was on.

Meanwhile back at Claire's house, her and Sanchez was in the midst of getting it in.

"Ooohh Baby, that feels so good!" Sanchez had his face buried deep in her box making her go crazy.

It's been so long since she's been pleased by anybody other than herself.

"Ooohh Right There Baby! Um Yes! Oh My God!"

Sanchez was a master at pleasing wit his tongue and he hasn't hit her wit the best part yet. He decided to see if she couldn't handle it. While licking her slowly, he started making his tongue twirl over her clit. When he did that, it sent her into a frenzy.

"Fuuuuck! Fuuuuck! Shiiit! Daaamn! Ooohh! Ooooh! Aaagghh! What are you doing to me! Oh My God I'm Cumming!!!

That's when I found out Claire was indeed a squirter. I slid up her body kissing her neck while grabbing a magnum off the nightstand. After putting it on, I slowly slid inside her.

"Aaagghh that feels so good, I haven't had sex in so long."

I began to put my sex game down on him. It's been a minute but I'm still that bitch and he's about to find out.

And for the next 45 minutes I had him saying shit he never thought he would say.

Three hours later we both were exhausted and knocked out.

"I needed that, a bitch almost forgot what it was like to have multiple orgasms."

CHAPTER 15

They Love This Work

"Hey Sis."

"Hey, how you feel this morning?"

"I feel good, jus got my back blew out."

"Ha! Ha! Ha!"

"You laughing and I'm dead serious."

"I know you are."

"So, did you let Sanchez knock tha cobwebs off that twat last night or what?"

"Bitch did I."

"Oh, Shit! Bout time, now you can put that toy up."

"Sis, he had a bitch all fucked up for a minute."

"Damn whip game vicious."

"Girl head game, tha best a bitch ever had."

"Oh shit."

"Yeah, he does his thing wit his tongue, that made a bitch nut so fast." We both started laughing.

"Shit, I'm gettin moist jus thinking about it," Claire said while slipping her hands into her panties to feel the moistness.

"Unh, Unh, Unh."

"Well, I hope you drained him this morning before he left."

"Yup, you better know it."

"So, I'm assuming you wifed up now?"

"No, we jus friends."

"Friends?"

"Yeah, wit Benefits."

"We'll see how long this lasts."

Meanwhile, on the block the junkies couldn't get enough of the new product. One Fein said he hadn't had any Coke this good since the 70s.

"That other work you had was good but it ain't got shit on this," another Fein said.

I knew it was only a matter of time before word of mouth traveled and all my spots will be doing double tha numbers we usually did.

"Yo Bro, you wasn't lying when you said it was way better than Los work."

"I got my Dover boy headed up for two at 26k."

"Why you ain't drop his number?"

"I did, I usually charge him 28,500."

"Oh a'ight."

"Plus, once he see what he can do wit it he'll be back for more."

"Shit at this rate I'll be hittin folk up later."

"Aye yo Sanchez."

"What up Lil' Dae-Dae?"

"For starters, drop tha Lil, it's jus Dae-Dae. You may not have noticed but I'm not little anymore."

"Oh, my bad Dae-Dae."

Cannon looked at Dae-Dae and then said, "I better put that in my mental rolodex."

"Thank you, can you grab some more, this shit damn near gone," he said handing Sanchez the bag.

"Damn that was a half of chicken worth of dimes."

"Look around Bro."

"Yeah, you better put that call in," he said reading a text.

"My Jersey folk hittin me for three, he's close, I'll be back after I handle him in Dover."

"A'ight, I'm going to go take care of that now."

"Dae-Dae you gone be kool til we get back."

"UAlready."

When I got to the spot I definitely had to hit Tayo, I only had four left. After four rings he picked up.

"What's up Tayo."

"I need to see you."

"So soon?"

"Yeah, they love this work."

"Same order?"

"Nah, Imma double it."

"OK."

"Matter of fact, add two more to that."

"No problem, if you give me an address I'll have it brought to you."

"You not bringing it?"

"No, I don't get my hands dirty unless I really have to."

"But don't worry, I trust him wit my life."

"A'ight," I said giving him the address.

"Give him 30 minutes."

"No problem, I'll be here."

Sure enough, in 30 minutes there was a knock on the door. (Knock-Knock) When I opened the door I was surprised to see a woman.

"Yes, may I help you?"

"Tayo?" is all she said.

"Please come in."

She put up a finger and then turned and went to retrieve what she left in her car. Once inside we exchanged bags.

"Thank you."

"No thank you."

And she left without another word. I called Tayo to let him know that everything was handled, and she was on her way back.

"No problem, I'll be waiting on your next call."

I pushed end knowing it would probably be a few weeks before I dump these, so I thought anyway. But once the word spread these chickens were flying the coop faster than I could count. Here I was taking over everybody's business, the ones I choose to deal with anyway.

4 days later, I was on tha phone with Tayo again.

"What it do Tayo?"

"Same shit different toilet."

"I need you."

"So soon?"

"I know right."

"Same order."

"Yeah, plus 20."

"You're not playing any games, are you?"

"I'm bout that bag."

"So, I see."

"Same spot."

"No problem 30 minutes."

Just like clockwork in 30 minutes there was a knock on the door. (Knock-Knock) I opened the door expected to see the same lady, but I got the shock of my life to see a lady who I definitely without a doubt in my mind knew was somebody's grandmother. We exchanged bags and she went on her merry way. I called to let Tayo know everything was good.

"OK. Hope my grandma didn't frightened you."

"Nah, jus surprise me though." We both laughed.

While I was in the lab my cousin from Philly called.

"Hello."

"What's up Lil' Cuz?"

"I can't call it. Please tell me it's some work down your end."

"What kind of work are we talkin?"

"Caine."

"Depends on what you talkin bout."

"Depends on tha numbers."

"And as you know tha number depends on how many."

"Well, I normally pay 21k but any more than 5 it drops to 19k."

I couldn't help but smile since I knew my cousin was not only lying but tryin to play me.

"Well Cuz, I hate to tell you, but you're never find it for that number here."

"Well what's tha number?"

"26k but anything more than three it's 24k."

"That's high."

"Cuz Imma be honest, my man tried to go up on me to 30k, so I found a new guy and tha work is so good you could turn 2 into 3 and tha work still be a 10.”

“Damn that’s good and that price way better than tha 28k I was really paying.”

“Hello Cuz, you still there?” I asked knowing he was.

“Yeah, I’m here, jus doing some math. Let me hit you right back, let me hit my partner to see what he wants to do.”

“Kool, no problem.”

I knew he was really calling everybody that was trying to score putting his number on it.

An hour later as I was about to walk out the door my Cuz hit me back. “Yo.”

“Cuz what’s tha best price you can get me 25 for?”

“600k.”

“That’s at 24k.”

“I know.”

“That’s tha best you can do?”

“Yup.”

“Damn a’ight, can I meet you at Aunt Jane’s crib? That’s half way for both of us.”

“How long?”

“I’m leaving now.”

“Kool, me too.” I called Sanchez, so he could drive the stash van. Cousin or not I was being cautious.

30 minutes later, I was pulling up at my aunt’s house at the same time as my Cuz. He got out with the duffle bag across his shoulder. He looked at

me like where's the work. I followed him up the steps while motioning for Sanchez to come on. Once inside I took my money counter out and proceeded to count his money.

"Damn you don't trust me Cuz?"

"This 600k Cuz, shit you used to count my 54k so why wouldn't I count this?"

"Good thing I did cause it was only 575k."

"You 25k light," I said looking him directly in his eyes.

"You sure Cuz."

"Nigga you jus watched me count it."

"Damn can I owe you that 25?" I laughed before saying no.

"Damn Cuz."

"Nigga I was short a punk ass 100 and you told me it was bizness."

"Don't worry about it, so I'll jus take one out."

"Hold up Cuz, I got some more spread on me."

He ran the money through until it hit 25k and then put the rest back in his pocket.

"It's always family," I said nodding my head.

"What's that supposed to mean?"

"Nuffin."

"A'ight, if it's what you say it is I'll be back in a few days."

DeAndre felt good knowing he just scored two bricks for himself and 46k, so in all actuality he paid 2 stacks for 3 bricks because he was definitely turning his 2 into 3.

Once back in Delaware at the stash spot Sanchez said he needed 10 total for his Dover and Jersey folk.

"Damn plus my folk need six that leaves nine."

"Shit, I know Tayo, like what tha Fuck he doing."

"Shit, he got that good work." Just as I was about to call him he called me.

"Cannon are you busy?"

"Nah, I was actually bout to call you."

"Is there a problem?"

"Actually, it is."

"What's wrong?" he asked with concerned in his voice.

"I need more, I'm down to 9."

"Oh," Tayo said relieved, "I thought I had to kill sum body."

"Nah."

"Can you meet me at Tessa's, I want to talk face-to-face."

"OK, I'll be there in 15 minutes."

"Me too."

"Sanchez handle your biz I got gotta meet Tayo."

"Kool."

CHAPTER 16

It's Time for Me to Branch Off

I pulled up at Tessa's at the same time as Tayo.

"This is why I like you, you're always on time."

"I used my key to let us in, I knew Tessa wasn't home because she called on her way to the nail salon."

"Would you like sum thing to drink?"

"A bottled water please." I handed him his water and sat down on the couch.

"Listen, I want to cut down on tha traffic to your spot. You've ran through 94 kilos in less than 2 weeks."

"I know and to be honest, I've never done that."

"I told you I normally do 10 to 12 hours a week, but this work is so good ery body wants it."

"I jus sold my cousin from Philly 25 at 24k."

"I thought."

"I know but he was taxing me when I was copping off him plus he grabbed everybody's money, so I'm sure he tax them."

"I see."

"Greed is a lot of people's biggest downfall."

"Yes, it is Cannon, yes, it is."

"Listen, from here on, I will match what you buy at tha same price you pay upfront."

"Wow, that's a bet."

"I'll take another 50 now. I have tha money in my car, you can take it wit you."

"OK." As we stood up Tessa came walking in.

"Well, well, well, if it isn't my two favorite guys, to what do I owe this pleasure."

"We were jus leaving," they both said and unison.

"Excuse me, I thought my favorite guys were waiting for me."

"Not this time."

"Cannon I'll be there in 45 minutes."

"Kool, I hit tha locks in back seat."

"Got you."

I can tell Tessa wanted to ask what we were talking about, so I said, "That wasn't about you."

"I didn't say it was."

"No, but you wanted to know."

"You think you know me."

"I know you enough." All she could do was laugh.

"Babe are you going to be busy later?"

"I don't know, why what's up?"

"I wanted to do sum thing."

"What and what time?"

"Maybe movies and dinner, I have to see what's playing and tha time."

"A'ight, jus hit my phone, I got to go."

"OK, I love you and be safe."

"Love you too."

Across town King was pissed for the past week his money had slowed down drastically and Cannon was to blame.

"I can't understand when he has tha same work that we do."

"Not King, I think he cut tha boy Los off and found a new connect."

"Yeah, but who?"

"Maybe he's fucking wit tha Gomez family."

"Damn I forgot about them."

"Don't Los fuck wit them though?"

"Nah, I think he got a Dominican line."

"Well, we need to find out cause damn everybody in tha city fuckin wit that work they got."

"I know, it might be time to start puttin in some work."

"Now that's what tha fuck I'm talking bout," Strap said clutching his .44 bulldog.

"Let me make these runs and you see what you can find out."

"Already on it." King slid behind the wheel of his Tahoe and pulled off.

"Fuck! Fuck! Fuck!" King yelled by banging on the steering wheel.

He had to figure out something and fast. It dawned on him, maybe he should send his Lil' Cuz to holla at Dae-Dae since they were boys. He could see what the numbers were and if they were reasonable have him cop a few.

30 minutes later he was pulling up on 30th to holla at Gotti.

"Yo, what it look like Lil' Cuz?"

"Shit I'll be ready for you later."

"No problem, I ain't come about that though."

"What up then?"

"You still Fuckin wit Dae-Dae?"

"Yeah, that's my nigga," he said looking at me crazy.

"You think you can hit him up to see what them things goin for."

I didn't need to hit him because I already knew since I was copping off him.

"Yeah, pull over, let me bust this trap."

King was my blood, but he didn't play fair ball. That's the reason I decided to flip his spread this time around plus that shit Dae-Dae got, got them going crazy around here. I walked up to the truck acting like I was on the phone with Dae-Dae.

"Yeah Bro, my folk want to know what tha math is on a bird." King shook his head which meant don't tell him it's me.

"26k, a'ight I'll let him know and hit you back."

"That's what I'm paying now so that's Kool. Can you grab me three of them if I get you tha paper?"

"Yeah, jus bring enough for two, I'll give you what I owe you by tha time you get back."

"I'll be back in bout a half."

"Kool, I'll be here." Soon as he pulled off I called Dae-Dae.

"What it do Gotti?"

"UAlready Imma need three in about a half."

"No problem, jus hit me, and we can meet at tha same spot as before."

"No problem, since you grabbin three I'll drop the number a dollar."

"Oh word? Fuck it, jus give me 5 then."

"Kool, waiting on you."

It was time for me to branch off and I do my own thing, especially since I couldn't get ahead fucking with King. Funny how your own blood will try and hold you back plus, overcharge you. I should have been hollering at Dae-Dae. Once I had King's spread, I hit Dae-Dae to let him know I was on my way.

"Damn you ain't playing Bro."

"Nah, I can't front, only two are mine, the other three are for my peeps, I'm charging him 26k."

"As you should, Gotti, you always keep it a bean; that's why you my Nigga for Life."

"Vice-versa, Imma be hollerin at you from now on."

"Kool, I'll look out as much as I can too."

"I know you will." By the time I made it back to King I could tell he was mad.

"Damn Nigga I thought I was going to have to send Strap after you." He was smiling but I knew he was dead serious and that just sealed it.

"Listen Cuz, I appreciate what you did for me, but Imma do my own thing from here." King looked at me as if I've lost my mind.

"What you saying Cuz?"

"I don't need you to front me no more work."

"Damn, I brought another two wit me for you since you was done."

"Nah I'm kool, I'll grab one off Dae-Dae," I said lying knowing I grabbed two.

"This mafucka tryin to play me," King thought to himself.

I knew what he was thinking so I said, "Listen Cuz, I don't think I'm tryin to play you. I do appreciate you helping me get my spread up, but I rather pay 26k than 30k any day. If it was you I know you would do the same shit."

He was definitely right about that but is still didn't change the fact I be losing out on money and another player to Cannon, even if not to him directly.

"It's kool Cuz, no sweat, keep doing you and be safe."

He lucky he's blood or Gotti would have definitely been taking a trip to the bone yard. Gotti watched King pull off thinking family or not, if he tries anything my auntie will be burying his Bitch Ass facts.

CHAPTER 17

I Gotta Feeling

Sanchez saw a figure creep up the block, so he grabbed his pistol from his waist. Just as he did he saw the guy pull out his pistol and let go. POP! POP! POP! POP!

He got out the way just in time as the first shot just missed his head but hit the pole that he was leaning against. Blocka, Blocka, Blocka, his 3rd shot hit the unknown man in the arm causing him to retreat. When the man yelled after being hit Sanchez recognized the voice but couldn't recall from where. He gave chase, but the man had a car waiting. Blocka, Blocka, Blocka, 3 more shots from his. 45 shattered the back window.

"Fuck!" Strap yelled once they were safely out of harm's way.

"Damn you got hit?"

"That bitch nigga grazed me."

"You good?"

"Yeah, I'm kool, ain't tha first time I've been grazed."

"We need to torch this car."

"I'll handle that, you jus get that arm bandaged up."

Back at the stash house Cannon, Dae-Dae, and Sanchez sat at the table engaged in a conversation about what had just transpired.

"Bro I don't know what that shit was about, I ain't beefin wit nobody."

"Now you see why I always say to stay on point?"

"I don't know why, but I gotta feeling King and his crew had a hand in this," Dae-Dae said with murder and his eyes.

"Calm down Lil' Bro, we need to make sure before we start busting our guns."

"Bro when I hit tha nigga and he screamed I know tha voice I jus got to figure out from were."

"Oh, you hittin him?"

"Yeah, it was only an arm shot though."

"I'm pretty sure that whoever it was is not gonna go to tha ER."

"We might jus have to sit back and let tha streets talk."

"Jus make sure that ery body is on full alert and holdin."

"Well, I'm bout to head back to tha block," Dae-Dae said while tucking his twin 9 in his waist.

"If you need us call."

"UAlready."

"I think we should stay off tha block til we find out what's going on."

"No disrespect Bro but you can, I'm not. I'm not letting nobody think they ran me off tha block." I don't even know why I said that.

"Truth be told, I thought it might have been one of Miguel's people." I looked at him as if to ask why he would think that.

"Oh shit, I never told you, did I?"

"Told me what?"

"That was my work."

"Huh?"

"Tha night them niggaz got killed."

"Naaah, you never told me you put a check on 'em."

"Cause I didn't, I put my own work in."

"Damn."

"I know you thought I was a pussy."

"Yeah, I thought you were soft."

"Come on Bro, you know it's a method to my madness. I had to make it seem like that to everybody so when I handle them niggas I'll be tha last person they expected."

"I have to admit, you had me pissed tha way you was letting him talk that bullshit."

"Didn't I tell you he will be on a T-shirt real soon?"

"I gotta find out who wanted me in tha boneyard and ASAP."

"What tha Fuck happin to your arm Scrap?"

"You wouldn't believe me if I told you."

"Oh yeah, told you about all that rough sex shit."

"You know I had Gotti grab me three bricks from Lil' Dae-Dae."

"Los ain't have shit?"

"Yeah, but I wanted to see what all tha fuss is about."

"What was tha ticket?"

"Same as Los."

"Right."

"Strap I can't front, whoever they Fuckin wit got that pure work."

"Oh yeah?"

"Yeah, look like some straight Columbia shit."

"I turned 3 into 4½ and tha shit is still better than Los shit."

"They Fuckin wit tha Gomez family King, I know it."

"Can't be Strap, that's who Los Fuckin wit."

"Then they got to have an out of town plug."

"Gotta be."

"You talk to Float today?"

"Nah, he been M.I.A. tha last few days."

"I tried to call him this morn, he ain't pick up."

"Hope he ain't back sniffing that shit."

"Me either."

"Time will tell."

"It always does Strap, it always does."

"So, what's tha deal wit you and home girl from Vanity?"

"Shit shorty kool."

"Yeah, her cousin hit me last night and wanted to do a movie and dinner, her treat."

"She has a nice head on her shoulders and she works as a realtor."

"Well, that's why you ain't get no ass that night."

"Why? She not no thot, she even apologize for leading me on that night. It was her first time out in a long time and the drinks had her tipsy."

"Shit more like drunk."

"I know, that's what I told her."

"Ha! Ha! Ha!"

"We supposed to get together tomorrow night."

"So, you are feeling her?"

"Anybody that makes her own money definitely has potential to be in my world."

"Your world huh?"

"But on tha serious note I need to find out who and where that work is coming from."

"That shit like that?"

"Yeah Strap, that shit is fire. If we can get our hands on that we can really Fuck this Shit up."

"King if you got an extra 1½ off that 3 and its still better than tha shit we got. It's definitely that work for sure."

"We might have to go through Gotti to grab that."

"I jus grabbed tha three to see what I could do wit it."

"I really don't want to give them niggaz my money on some real shit."

"We can dump what we got and then grab a nice amount and hopefully by tha time we done we'll know sum thing."

"I hope so."

SHERATON DOWNTOWN WILMINGTON...

"Damn Baby save a little bit for me," the prostitute said looking at Floats sniff the whole bag of heroin.

"Don't worry about it Baby there's plenty more where that came from."

"Give me some."

"You got to work for it first." Float pulled a bag out to entice her.

"Why you teasing me Daddy."

"I'm not." She pulled Floats penis out of his boxers and her eyes got big as a softball.

"Daaamn, I ain't never seen a penis this big and it's not even hard yet."

"You not scared of it are you?"

Her mouth said no but her eyes told a different story. Float sprinkled a little bit of the heroin on his man. She snorted it off with the quickness and then begun to lick the residue, once she did that it began to grow.

"Damn this shit look like and elephants' trunk," she thought to herself, *"Imma need a lot more of that heroin if he thinks he puttin that up in me."*

As if on cue Float tossed her 3 more bags that she quickly scarfaced. Between the heroin and the liquor, she was feeling good and horny the thought of sitting on that mandingo had her wet. Before she could Floats phone started ringing. He looked at it and then pushed ignore. He been doing this all day, if it wasn't King, then it was Strap. He just didn't feel like being bothered with them right now.

"Now, where were we?"

Without saying a word, she put the tip in and then wiggled her body until half of it was inside her.

"AAAGGHH SHIT Daddy!"

"Take this pipe girl, take it!"

Before long she had my whole shit in her taking it like the true champ she was.

After about 45 minutes, she was releasing her load. 30 seconds later, I was doing the same thing. We both collapsed on the bed and 2 minutes later we were both snoring.

CHAPTER 18

Miguel's Funeral

"Did you find out anything Mom?"

"I'm afraid not Miguel was out in tha streets going crazy." Cinco and Trans both looked at their mom, but before either could say anything.

"I know you both told me that, but I didn't want to face tha truth."

"It could have been anybody who did this Mom."

"I have to get some rest, so I can bury my son tomorrow." Cinco and Trans both hugged and kissed Amelia before leaving her bedroom.

Once in the hallway Trans asked, "Where do we start?"

"I really don't know Trans."

Miguel's funeral was packed, and I think most people came to make sure he was really dead. Amelia sat in the front row with her dark shades on in deep thought. Memories flooded her mind of Miguel. Amelia wouldn't let them see her weak, so she held her tears back for as long as she could. As soon as they closed Miguel's casket, she lost it.

"Noooo my Miguel, open that casket! Why did you take my son? Who did this to you?"

When none of her questions were answered she swore on his dead body she would get the answers to all of her questions one way or another. Anybody that knew Amelia Gomez knew she would indeed get those answers. The pall bearers carried him out to his final resting spot. Long after everyone was gone, Amelia and her sons remained.

"Mother we are about to unleash terror on this city until we get tha answers we need."

Amelia took her shades off, so she could look at both her sons as she spoke.

"Be smart about what you are about to do, we don't want or need tha heat on us. So, move smart, don't let your emotions override your intellect."

With that being said, they also said their final goodbyes and made their way to the Limo. All the while a tinted-out Chevy Impala sat off to the side watching the whole thing as if it was a movie. Once the Limo was gone the Chevy pulled up to the grave site. The driver slowly got out walking to the grave wit one quick motion he dropped down into the grave. Lifting up the casket he stared into the face of Miguel.

"I'll see you in Hell," he said.

SPTT, SPTT, SPTT, SPTT putting 4 bullets in Miguel's face.

"I was robbed of killing you, so this will have to do it SPTT, SPTT," he said putting 2 more in his face and climbing back out of his grave.

He walked back to his car as if he didn't just put 6 bullets in a dead man's face. He unscrewed the silencer and tucked the pistol back into his waist. HE LOOKED IN HIS REAR-VIEW MIRROR AND THOUGHT *"NOW THAT'S HOW YOU SEND A MUTHA FUCKA OFF FLOAT."*

CHAPTER 19

Miguel Is Dead

"Why is this mall so crowded today?"

"They must be having a sale or sum thing."

"Ain't nowhere to park."

"She's comin out right there."

"I see her." After we parked we went into tha mall to do some shopping.

"Let's go in H & M since we're right here."

"Yeah, they definitely got a sale going, look how long that Damn line is."

Clare couldn't help but to laugh when she saw Smoke her old boyfriend standing in line with his baby mother.

"What you laughing at?" Tessa asked.

As soon as Tessa turned around she knew exactly what she was laughing at.

Tessa being Tessa, she walked over, "Hey Smoke."

"Hey Tara."

"What's up Tessa."

"Heeey Tessa."

"Damn she got big," Tessa said referring to their daughter.

"Yes, Girl and bad as Shit."

"How old is she now?"

"Three."

Smoke was looking at Claire who didn't even bother to look his way.

"Well, it was nice seeing y'all."

"You too."

"Bitch you crazy."

"What? I wanted to see tha baby that destroyed his happy home."

Even though it was 3 years ago I knew Claire still felt some type of way about it. Shit I would too if my man cheated and had a baby at that. They were working through the infidelity part, it was when Tara said she was pregnant that's when all Hell broke loose.

"I can't believe they're together."

"I can, Smoke is not tha type to abandon his child. He always said he thinks a child needs both parents. Well, he looks happy."

"Bitch, he couldn't stop staring at you."

"You know that saying, tha one tha guy got away."

Bitch Sanchez better capitalized."

At the Mention of his name Claire was all smiles.

"Damn Bitch let me find out."

"Find out what?"

"I said his name and all I saw was pearly whites."

"That's my boo."

"Unh, Unh, Unh, you whipped."

"No, I'm jus happy Sis."

"You deserve to be."

After we paid for our things we decided to walk to Forever 21.

"Hey, if it ain't my fav couple, what's up Jerz, hey Tam."

"What's up Tessa."

"Hey Tess."

"I jus read your latest books Who Can You Trust and Bonded by DNA."

"That's what's up, thanks for tha support, I definitely appreciate it."

"You're very talented, keep up tha good work."

"I got a few more bout to drop so be lookin for them."

"Yup."

"A'ight y'all."

"Yo they been together since I was born."

"Bitch you dumb."

"For real, that got 20 in at least."

"Yeah, I respect that, and he wouldn't dare cheat."

"I haven't read his books, but I heard they're good."

"They are and he gettin money off of 'em."

"He always got at a bag from what I heard."

"Yeah, but now he's getting that legal bag."

"That's what's up, I like when a Muthafucka switch over."

After we leave out of here I'll go next door to Barnes and Noble and get his books."

"It's not as crowded in here as H&M."

"Thank God."

We grabbed a few things and then headed next door. After a few minutes we located the urban section.

"He got three books out."

"Yeah, Betrayal & Deceit been out though."

"Oh, reading tha back it sounds good."

"Bitch Zoey that bitch."

"Ha! Ha! Ha!"

"You hype or nah?"

"He need to drop part 2 for that facts."

"Let me pay for these so I can get me some Suki."

"I can go for some of that myself."

"I need to go around to Sneaker Villa and see if they got those Jordan 9's."

"I heard Sanchez say sum thing bout those."

"Yeah, that's what Cannon wants."

After striking gold at the Villa with the J's it was time to put some food in our bellies.

"They gon to be siked."

"I know, I jus hope they didn't already get 'em."

"If I know Cannon he didn't."

"Well, if Sanchez did, he'll have two pair cause a bitch ain't bringing 'em back."

"Shit I know that's right."

We ordered our food and decided to eat in the Food Court since we were so hungry.

"This Honey Chicken and Shrimp is tha bomb."

"Yeeees!"

"Imma grab me one of those Chicken Teriyaki Steaks from Charlie's for later."

"Imma get some more of this wit tha rice instead of noodles."

"I better get Cannon sum thing since I'm not cooking tonight."

"Bitch you gon make a good wife."

"You think so?"

"I know so."

"Come let's get this food and get outta here."

Just as we reached the car a horn honked. We both looked to see who it was, but it was just somebody wanting to know if we were leaving.

"I'm thinking about trading this in and getting me sum thing else."

"Ain't nuffin wrong wit this one."

"I know, but I've had it for the past 3½ years and I'm thinkin about getting tha Infiniti truck."

"Now those are nice and tha price is reasonable."

"I know, it jus depends on how much they gon give me on this when I trade it in."

"Well, considering tha miles are low and it is in great condition, you gon to get sum thing nice."

"That's what I'm hoping."

"Especially since it's an Infinity too."

"I'll see Saturday when I go."

"You know I'm going, a bitch might see sum thing I like."

"Well, you better bring your checkbook."

Across town in a basement Cinco and Trans had Pete tied up and blindfolded.

"Where am I?"

Cinco snatched off his blindfold. Pete tried to adjust his eyes to the light, he started to see two images out of the eye that wasn't swollen.

"What tha Fuck is this about?"

"You know exactly what it's about." The only thing that comes to mind was the five racks that he owed King.

"Yo, did King send you?"

"King? No, my friend but Amelia did." Pete was puzzled now.

"Why would she send for me?"

"Simple, Miguel."

"I don't owe Miguel anything."

"Why did you kill him?"

"Kill him?"

"Yeah."

"Listen, I jus got back in town last night, I didn't even know Miguel was dead."

"You had beef wit him, yes?"

"Man, that beef been squashed months ago, in fact, I was buying my Shit off of him." Trans looked at Cinco.

Cinco then said, "If this was true, how did it come packaged?"

Pete explained it to them detail for detail and once he did they knew he was telling tha truth."

"Untie him."

"When did this happen?"

"Last week." Pete pulled his phone out to show them a text.

"Hey Bro, Imma need you soon I get back in town next week."

"A'ight no problem, I'll be ready for you."

"Sorry about the misunderstanding."

"Yeah, we jus want to find tha person or persons responsible."

"What was Miguel charging you?"

"26k."

"A'ight, take my number and hit me; I'll do bizness wit you at tha same number."

"Kool, I need three now."

"I'll call you in an hour and tell you where to come and I'll have sum thing extra for this," he said pointing to Pete's eye.

Pete was already plotting his revenge; never could they think they would get away with this and live.

CHAPTER 20

Business Going Extremely Well

"What it do Gotti?"

"I can't call it."

"I need you to get at Lil' Dae-Dae."

"He jus goes by Dae-Dae now."

"A'ight, whatever floats his boat."

"What you trying to do?"

"I need 10, think he can handle that?"

"Pretty sure he can, he handled my 5."

"Damn you doing ya thing."

"Yeah, thanks to you and that work he got."

"I see," King said looking at all the traffic that was flowing.

"Let me hit him real quick." After about 3 rings he picked up.

"What up Homie?"

"You, my folk need a dime."

"When?"

"Now if you ready."

"A'ight, you know where to meet me."

"No doubt, on my way."

"Grab that off tha back seat."

"Kool, I'll be right back." By the time I got there Dae-Dae was just pulling up.

"Damn ya peeps grabbing like that?"

"Man, if I told you who this was for you wouldn't believe me."

"Try me."

"King."

"Nah, thought he had a look?"

"He do but it ain't Fuckin wit this no doubt. But check it, after this, don't bring that nigga paper."

"No problem, if I wasn't making 10 bands off him he wouldn't be getting this."

"Are you hittin him?"

"Damn right, tha way he was taxing me."

"It's only right, jus tell him from now on I'm waiting."

"I got you Bro."

"Damn, what tha Fuck you was doing?" King questioned.

"You a favor."

"Took long enough Nigga."

"Check this out King, I'm not either one of those two niggaz you run wit so please stop talkin to me like that." King could hear the threat in his voice.

"Yo, Imma act like I ain't hear that."

"You can act like it if you want, but I said what I said," I said tossing the bag through the window and stepping off.

"My aunt might jus be burying a son real soon," King said pulling off.

Bitch Ass Nigga," Gotti said as King rode pass.

If looks could kill they both be dead right now.

At the stash house Dae-Dae was putting his quarter mill he just made off of King up when Cannon and Sanchez walked in.

"You niggaz will never guess or believe who jus spent a quarter mill."

"Who?"

"King."

"Huh?"

"My man Gotti who be spending came for him."

"I told him not to come for him no more."

"Yeah, Fuck that bitch nigga."

"Los must have cut him off."

"Nah, he jus wants this work."

"Well, he better make them 10 last."

"If I had known they was for him from jump he wouldn't have got shit."

"Gotti should've taxed his punk ass."

"You know he did, shit he even said if it wasn't for tha 10 bands he was making off him he wouldn't have even called. Ha! Ha! Ha!"

"I don't blame him, shit a free 10 bands, who wouldn't do that."

"I heard tha Gomez Brothers snatched ya boy Pete up."

"Oh yeah?"

"Yeah, few nights ago."

"Well, he's still alive, I jus saw him a few hours ago at Frank's on tha hill."

"I think they was askin bout his beef he had wit Miguel."

"They squashed that beef," Sanchez said.

"Yeah, he was even copping off him since then."

"Guess that's why he's still alive."

"Ain't no way a muthafucker goin to grab me up and not kill me and still be living."

"Bro if I know Pete them niggaz is living on borrowed time; you can bet best believe that."

"They gotta lot of niggaz to snatch up then," Cannon said looking at Sanchez.

"Let 'em try it," he said showing his pistol.

"Jus as you always do, stay on point."

Dae-Dae looked at Sanchez, "You think that other shit was them?"

"Nah, that nigga was trying to get me tha Fuck outta here."

"Still no word on that Shit yet?"

"Nah, oh trust you'll know when I find out sum thing."

"Cannon you need to reach out to your folk, once I take these 6 it's only going to leave us wit 20."

"No problem, I already put tha order in."

Sanchez said, "I got my Dover and Jersey Boys comin through in bout an hour, so I need that last dub."

"Damn, Imma take that now but by tha time your peeps come through that fresh batch will be here."

"Kool."

"Yo Big Bro we all got a few heavy hitters, so it might be time to step up tha order."

"Already a few ahead of you Dae-Dae." I looked at my watch and as if on cue there was a knock on the door.

"I got it, hey come in."

When Sanchez and Dae-Dae saw the old lady walk in they both had that what the Fuck face. She sat both duffle bags down, took the one I handed her and said thanks then left back out. They both started bagging up.

"What's so funny?"

"Man, that's sum body grandma."

"Hey Bro, tha less attention tha better."

"Yup, now grab those while I punch this code in."

To the average eye it looks like an alarm which it was but to us it was double as the stash spot. After hitting the required numbers, the retractable floor slid back revealing the 20 kilos and money that set inside.

"Leave 40 in one bag."

By the time they finished there was 180 neatly wrapped kilos inside the stash spot.

"Close that up and let's get up outta here."

Sanchez took his 20 and we all went our separate ways. Business was going extremely well, I had reached heights I never could even imagine thanks to Tessa's introduction to her father.

By the time I finished it was still early, so I decided to head to the crib and spend some time with Tessa.

"Hey Babe," I yelled out walking into the house.

"Hey Baby, I'm in tha bedroom."

"You goin somewhere?"

"No, I jus got out of the shower bout to put on my nightgown. I see sum body is happy to see me," she said referring to my hard on that was very visible.

"Ha! Ha! Ha! I guess he is."

"Those are for you," she said pointing to the Sneaker Villa bag that's by the closet door.

As soon as I seen the Jordan box I got hype.

"Oh shit, I couldn't find these anywhere, me or Sanchez."

"What you smiling for."

"Cause Claire got him a pair too."

"Did y'all get these from Sneaker Villa at tha mall?"

"Yeah."

"We went there, and they said two females jus got tha last two pair in our sizes. Never did I think they were talking about you and Clare Bear."

"I heard you talkin about them, I was jus hopin you didn't get 'em."

"Nah, and I was pissed too."

"Well, don't worry I had ya back Baby."

"You always do."

"That's why you love me," she said puckering up?

"And you know it," I said giving her a nice kiss.

"I bought you sum thing to eat from tha mall cause I wasn't cooking tonight."

"Kool."

"It's in tha microwave so when you come back in."

"Damn you rushing me out. What you got company comin over?"

"Cannon stop disrespectin me."

"I'm jus saying I was going to take a shower and stay in wit you." Tessa started smiling hard.

"Well, go get in tha shower, then we can eat and cuddle."

"Sounds like a winner to me."

By the time I got out of the shower and put my pj's on Tessa had my food heated up on a plate waiting for me. Once we were done we got in bed and surfed through the channels.

"Baby see what new movies they got on tha Fire stick."

"You do it, I don't know how to work that Shit," I said handing her the remote control.

"Let's watch Kevin's Hart What Now."

I didn't care what she was going to watch because I knew I would be sleep in a few minutes anyway, unless she felt frisky. Tessa put the remote on the nightstand and then slid over laying her head on my chest. I knew Cannon was sleep by the way his chest was moving up and down. It felt so good laying there, I didn't even want to get up and use the bathroom. While on my way, my phone started to ring. I quickly answered it, so it did not wake Cannon.

"What's up Sis? Shit I was laying in tha bed."

"Me too."

"My Baby decided to come home early tonight."

"Damn Sanchez came over early tonight too."

"Guess he wanted some of that good good."

"Bitch he knocked out."

"Ha! Ha! Ha!"

"What's up? Why you laughing?"

"Cannon is knocked out too, but a Bitch need a fix, so I'll be waking him up after while."

"Yup, so was I."

"Nothing like waking up to some blazing head."

"Bitch you ain't never lied."

"Hey Cannon, was like a little kid when he saw those Jordans."

"Sanchez too talkin bout him and Cannon searched everywhere for them."

"Oh yeah, I meant to call you earlier."

"For what?"

"I saw Homegirl from tha nail salon."

"Who?"

"The one that kept staring."

"Did you? Where you see her at?"

"Fresh Grocer."

"Bet she was staring again."

"Yup, so I asked her did she know me from somewhere."

"What she have to say?"

"She asked if I used to mess wit Mike?"

"Huh?"

"Yup, it was his sister she said she remembered me from tha pictures he had at her house. She wanted to ask me at tha nail salon but didn't know if it was me or not. Shit, I would rather her asked then jus keep staring tha way she was."

"I know right?"

"Well, I'll call you tomorrow."

"A'ight."

I put my phone back on the nightstand and snuggled back up with my baby. It was only 11 o'clock so I decided to let him get some more sleep.

CHAPTER 21

A Better Profit

Never had King seen a better profit then you he did off that work from Dae-Dae. He turned 10 into 15 with no problems or complaints and now that he was getting low he needed to reach out to Gotti. *The number you called is no longer in service.)* He dialed again to make sure he dialed the right number only to get the same results. King didn't think anything because in this game it was common to change your number. If he only knew he was the sole reason for Gotti changing his number.

"Damn, let me slide up on him since I'm already over this way," he said to himself.

When he pulled up he couldn't believe the traffic flow, it was heavier than last time.

"Yo Cuz." Gotti continued to talk to one of his young boys.

"Yo Cuz," King said wit more base in his voice.

"What up?"

"You ain't hear me?" King asked clearly agitated.

"I heard you, but I was handling sum thing."

"What up wit Dae-Dae?"

"He dry right now, I jus hollered at him. Can you sell me a few."

"Nah, cause I ain't got 'em at that number."

"Well, what number you got 'em at?"

"30."

"Daaamn Cuz, it's me." Gotti had to stop himself from laughing in Kings face.

"That's tha same Shit I was saying to you."

"Cuz that was way different, you wasn't spending ya paper, I am."

"That's tha best I can do, plus he said he don't know when he goin to be ready."

"Shit!" *King thought about it, that's 300k for 10 if he even can cover that.*

"Damn you rough Cuz, I'll be back in 20 minutes, let me go grab tha spread."

"A'ight, I'll be right here waiting on you."

Gotti thought about stretching the work and then decided against it, especially since I would be a free 50 stacks he would be making off him. Instead he called Dae-Dae to see if he could get up with him in the next hour.

When King pulled back up Dae-Dae motioned for his young boy to bring the work.

"It's tha same shit, right?"

"Come on Cuz."

"Jus makin sure."

"Respect." I grabbed the spread and headed to my car, so I could meet Dae-Dae.

A few blocks away on 24th and Carter, Float was talking cash shit, and to anybody else they would think he was crazy.

"Nigga ya Cowboys ain't going to no Damn Super Bowl."

"Who can stop us in tha NFC?"

"Let's bet a friendly nickel they don't make it."

"Nah, but we can bet 200 if you want."

"Fuck it, bettin sum thing is a lot better then nothing."

"We can bet 500 ya bum ass Birds don't even make tha damn playoffs."

"That's OK, we'll be back strong next year."

"Man y'all say that every year and every year it's tha same Shit."

"Yo Nigga, what tha deal is?" Strap asked Float pulling up with King riding shotgun.

"I can't call it."

"Fuck you been this past week?"

"Up top," Float said with a smile.

"Philly?"

"Yeah, I got a bad shorty up there, she had a nigga hostage."

"Why you ain't answer tha phone?"

"Man, I lost that Shit."

King was calling it to see if it would ring or if he really had indeed lost it. It was ringing but he definitely didn't have it.

Strap was looking to see if he saw any traces of Float getting high.

"What you doin?"

"Finishing off what I had before shorty kidnapped a nigga. I'm thinkin bout opening shop up on her block. It's money but nobody got a steady plug so it's a free for all."

"How you know this?"

"Observing plus her little brother was sayin it."

"You need to make sure before you jus try to open up shop."

"I am believe that."

"You need to get a new phone."

"I'm bout to do that in a few minutes."

"A'ight we goin slide back through later."

"He didn't look like he was high."

"Nah, and he didn't have his phone either."

"How you know?"

"I called it."

"Did you get some more of that from Dae-Dae?"

"Nah."

"Damn they got spoiled wit that."

"I know but Gotti sold me some."

"Oh, that's what's up."

"Fuck, that nigga charged me 3k a kilo."

"Damn but you ain't have a choice."

"I know cause he said he don't know when Dae-Dae gon be ready."

"We need to find out where they gettin that shit from."

"Shit that's what I been doin but wit no results."

"Los is supposed to drop tha number."

"That would be love."

"Tha Shit I get from Los I knock off in weight sales but tha Shit that I grab from Dae-Dae straight to tha block wit it."

"I rode through 30th yesterday, I see Gotti got that shit jumpin around there."

"Yeah, I noticed today when I was up there."

"Might need to send my young boys through there and lay everybody down."

That might not be a bad idea, so they assumed. Little did they know they be in for one Hell of surprise when and if they ever did.

CHAPTER 22

Your Product

"Tayo this is my best friend Sanchez but we're more like brothers."

"Nice to finally put a face wit the name I hear so much about," Sanchez said while extending his hand.

"Like wise," Tayo said in return while shaking his hand.

"So tha reason I wanted to meet wit you is to let you know your friend King has been asking a lot of questions concerning where you are getting your product."

"Nobody knows that, so we don't have to worry about him ever finding that out."

"That is true, but my concern is he may try to have you followed to see if he can catch you in tha act."

"We are both very cautious when we move."

"Yes, you are. That little situation you had," he said looking at Sanchez, "I believe it was King's right-hand man." Sanchez thought back to the scream when he shot him.

"Mutha Fucka!" he yelled causing everyone to look at them.

"Calm down."

"Sorry but I knew, I knew that voice when I shot him."

"You have to play it smart, don't act off emotions, you will get him soon enough."

"Trust me, when I tell you Tayo, I will never act off emotions. I'm a very patient man."

"I know, this is why Amelia is wit out her precious Miguel." Cannon and Sanchez both looked at each other.

"Trust me, there isn't too much I don't know about."

"We see," they both said in unison.

Sanchez thought back to the night where there was nobody out so how could he even know that was him?

"I will make sure that everything on my end is secure as well."

"I can see King's days are coming to an end. Kinda wish you would have ended his life that day in that alley huh?"

"Damn you wasn't lying, you know it all."

"I try to know all there is to know, so I can be on top of everything. Now if you will excuse me, I have another meeting. No need to get up, stay and finish, lunch is on me," he said putting a hundred-dollar bill on the table before walking out.

"Yo Bro, how tha Fuck did he know all that?"

"He's a resourceful guy."

"Well, I'm glad he's on our side."

"Who you Tellin, me too."

On some real, I couldn't figure out for the life of me where I knew that voice from but now I know.

"Bro that nigga dead and I put that on my life. We gon take everything from them, we'll take they life last."

"Sounds like a plan, Imma do my little homework, give me bout a week, I'll know everything we need to know about them bitch ass niggaz."

"Come on let's get out of here."

We both reached in our pockets and threw 20's on the table with the hundred that Tayo had left.

"Hold up guys ya check."

"No need, tha money is on tha table keep tha change."

When she got to the table and counted the money we left, after taking what the bill was she had a tip of $180. She was more than happy.

Once we got back to the hood it was jumping like any other day.

"Fuck this Shit!"

"What up Bro?" Sanchez walked over to where King's people were standing.

"Yo, check this out." Dae-Dae slid over as well.

"What's up Homie," one of them said.

"Y'all out here pumpin for King, right?"

"Yeah."

"Kool, check this out, no more of his work will be sold out here; you can tell him Sanchez said so."

"What's this about Homie?"

"I jus decided since we...," he said pointing to me and Dae-Dae, "since we built this Shit, it's only fair that we get it all."

"Come on Homie, y'all gettin 90% of tha paper anyway."

"You're right but why should we settle for 90 when we can get tha whole 100?"

"I don't want no beef wit y'all. Matter fact, you can call King, I'll tell him myself." One of the guys pulled his phone out and called King.

"Yo Lil' Homie, I'm bout to pull up on you in 5 minutes."

"Kool."

"Well, that's even better, I'd rather talk face-to-face."

I slid across the street to get my .44 out the car just in case it got messy. King was pulling up just as I was shutting my door. I decided to stay over here but I could hear them clear as day.

"What's up, what's tha deal?"

"I was jus explaining to ya folk that this is over."

"Fuck you mean?"

"Just what tha Fuck I said, this love affair is over. No more of ya product will be sold on our block. We revived this block and we let your boys post up for tha past few months, but that shit is over. On some real, if it wasn't for Cannon it would've never happened to begin wit facts."

"Sanchez, I hear and feel what you're sayin but truthfully I ain't try'n to hear that Shit."

"Well, so you sayin that they can be replaced."

"I guess you can say that," Strap said now stepping out the truck with his gun in hand.

"Don't even reach for it. I think it might behoove you to put that away," Cannon said standing behind Strap.

"Now you see fellas, we could have handled this a whole different way, but out of tha respect I had for y'all we chose to call you up and talk like men. King let's be honest, if I had tried to put any of my peoples on ya blocks they would probably be dead. So, jus respect tha fact that we let them stay this long. Then Strap you get out wit your pistol for what?"

"I didn't like where it was going. Ha! Ha! Ha!"

"What if I would've jus walked up on you and put ya Shit all over this pretty white truck jus cause I didn't like tha fact that one of you pulled out and two you said these guys are replaceable. Which tells me you don't care if they live or die. See fellas and these are tha guys you work for, wow. I actually like you guys and that is why bullets didn't fly only conversation."

I could see the one they called Dink staring at King and Strap wit pure hatred in his eyes, at that point I knew I could get him to join our team.

"Damn Strap, to think I actually respected you," Dink said.

"What Nigga?" But before Strap could pull his heat Dink already had his drawn.

"Don't make me do it, I don't got or want no beef wit you. I'm jus not Fuckin wit you niggaz no more. I may be a lot of things, but a fool is not one, you niggaz showed your true colors today."

King spoke up, "Listen, you can do what you want as long as you got my spread."

"Ha! Ha! Ha! You got to be crazy if you think I'm giving you Shit."

"Yeah Homie, you can chalk that up. There's always loses in tha game and this be one of 'em," both Preme and Jason said.

King knew that all three of them would let their hammers blow, that was part of the reason he put them out here.

"Oh, you niggaz will pay."

"Please don't make any threats cause you might not leave here tha way you came," Dink said cutting Strap off.

Strap knew he was dead serious, so he just said, "You got that Homie. Now get back in ya truck and pull off."

King was so heated, he never been played like Preme, Jason, and Dink just played him, this was far from over. He knew that Cannon wouldn't let them continue to hustle out there, so they would have to go back to Jersey and he would most likely pay them a visit.

"Listen Cannon, we meant no disrespect."

"None was taken, that had everything to do wit them not y'all."

"We not try'n to cut in on your money but is there any way we could purchase some work?"

"Yeah, cause on some real, we was about to ask what tha number was on tha whole one anyway. Only thing is we were going to pay him his money and do our own thing."

"Listen, I don't have a problem wit you grabbin from us and doing ya thing but tha decision is theirs," I said pointing to Sanchez and Dae-Dae.

"As long as you're coppin from us I don't care, it's still money in tha pot."

"Respect, say no more. When can we get that?"

"Whenever you want it and it's 25k."

"Damn that's a sweet number, give us two at that price. That nigga was raping us at 32k."

"Damn, he was straight raping y'all. Greed is always tha motive."

"Yeah, greed will get you slumped too."

"I've seen greed get many people killed, so you're absolutely right about that."

"Better watch those two though," Dae-Dae said, "he was always on tha block, so he had developed a half ass friendship wit Preme, Dink, and Jason. It was more of a respect thing. Tha thing about King is he's not built for war."

"I know, I saved his life on a few occasions."

"You sure did," Dink said wit a murderous look, "you only can play off tha safe for so long. We about money, but if you cross that line as King and Strap jus did, then it is what it is."

"A'ight well, I'm bout to handle that for y'all, I'll be back in 45 minutes," Sanchez said.

"Kool, we'll be here wit tha spread by tha time you get back."

"Cannon let me catch a ride."

"Sure."

"Yo Bro I thought tha boy Dink was going to kill them niggaz right there."

"He was but I shook my head no cause we don't need that kind of heat on tha block."

"Them niggaz had a lot of nerve to say they were replaceable."

"I don't respect that move."

"Anybody that is a part of your team deserves tha same respect as tha rest of ya team."

"King plays checkers not chest."

"I'm tha Plug really I'm tha Plug."

"Fuck this nigga want? Yo," I said putting my phone on speaker.

"What's up My Friend, I haven't heard from you in a while."

"Things happen."

"I got Grade A work at 30k."

"Ha! Ha! Ha! You joking right?"

"No, My Friend it's tha best out there."

"I seriously doubt that."

"You're insulting me wit that number Los."

"30k is good when everyone is charging 32k."

"Why would I pay you 30k when you only pay 21k." This caught Los by surprise that he knew what he was paying.

"My Friend, I wish it was that great for me."

"It has to be, you charge my competition 26k, you know he has a big mouth." Los knew this to be true and King spent nowhere what Cannon spent.

"He lies to you, he pays 30k."

Cannon didn't believe him and at this point he could care less what he was charging him or anybody else.

"How much you paying now My Friend?" Cannon looked at Sanchez and mouthed watch this.

"Los you would not believe me if I told you."

"Try me."

"Half of what you want."

"Bullshit my friend."

Told you that you wouldn't believe me."

"And you were right."

"My guy is in Texas," Cannon said lying.

Los now believed him that he had a guy in Texas who had that same price. Only problem was Los didn't have the means to get it here and he surely wasn't taking the risk.

"Yo you still there?"

"I am here."

"Yo since you pay so much I could give them to you at 20k but if you grab 50 or more I can do 19k." This really made Los mad.

"Who does he think he is?"

"Well, I'm in tha middle of bizness, hit me when and if you want to do bizness," Cannon said then pushed end without letting him respond.

"Ha! Ha! Ha! Yo, I know he salty."

"Fuck him."

"Would you sell him 50 for that price?"

"Sure, that's a quick 50k profit for us."

Los still couldn't believe Cannon had just talked to him like that. Los thought about it because truth to be told, he didn't have nowhere near the money to purchase 50 kilos. He spent his money just as fast as he made it. He didn't even have any clients that bought that at most 20 to 25.

CHAPTER 23

The Beat Down

"Yo Imma lay all them niggaz down," Strap said with venom and his voice.

"Be kool Bro, they're expecting us to do that. We going to let it blow over then catch them wit their pants down."

"You right Bro, I'm jus so pissed."

"Me too, and those niggaz think they gonna keep my Fuckin money? I ain't never let a nigga take Shit from me and live to talk about it. Imma hold off sending them wolves through too. When we go through there it'll be like a tornado."

"I talked to Float earlier he up top laying tha groundwork."

"If we can open a block up there I see big things in our future."

"Who you telling?"

"We need to slide through to see what it look like."

"I'll let him know we gon come through tomorrow."

BLOCKA, BLOCKA, BLOCKA

Strap and King ducked as bullets started to fly. POP POP POP POP POP, TAT TAT TAT, TAT TAT TAT, BLOCKA BLOCKA, BOOM BOOM, BOC BOC BOC BOC. There are so many different guns going off King thought he was in Iraq. When the shots stopped, they both came out from behind the car.

"Noooo!"

Was the sound they heard as they saw Dame laid out with a hole the size as a golf ball in his head still clutching his pistol. Another girl took his pistol out of his hand.

"Key-Key, Fuck was that about?"

"That was them Westside boys they've been beefing wit."

"Them niggaz laid some heavy shit."

"Let's get outta here before them boys show up."

"Yeah, cause Dame gone, so it's going to be hot as Hell over here for a sec."

"Damn R.I.P. Lil' Homie."

We pulled off just in time; police started coming from everywhere.

*"I See Death Around tha Corner...*Turn this up Bro! This song always put me in a zone and I definitely see death around the corner. *I See Death Around tha Corner Gotta Stay High to Survive.* Damn this my Shit."

"You know that shit gonna slow tha money up on tha block for a while."

"I know but we got other spots, so it won't affect us."

"Did you ever get up wit Gotti?"

"Yeah, but I'm not going to keep payin 30K."

"I feel you but tha extra five more than makes up for it."

"Yeah, you right, it's jus tha fact he thinks he's getting one off on me."

"We need that shit on that Philly block."

"That's what Float got, he put it all in jars."

"Damn, that's gonna be a Hell of a profit."

"He got shorty's brother runnin that shit."

"Smart move."

"Imma hit tha bar and have me a drink or two. What you bout to get in to?"

"You can drop me at my whip, I'm bout to slide through shorty's spot."

"Y'all been kickin it a lot."

"Yeah, she kool people wit out tha added stress."

"I feel you on that, these streets stressful enough wit out a broad adding more stress."

"There you go."

"I'll hit you up in tha morn."

"Kool, be safe."

"Always my nigga always."

When King walked into the Casbar he spotted Tess and Claire. He really wasn't in the mood for conversation, so he just gave them a head nod and then made his way to an empty stool.

"Bitch that's a first."

"What?"

"King ain't come in all up in a bitch face."

"You know tha boy Dame from his block got killed tonight."

"Nah, I didn't know, that explains tha long face. Was they still beefing wit those young boys from West Side?"

"Yup, that's who they said did it."

"They probably beefin over nothing."

"More than likely, definitely ain't about no money."

"When they gon to learn."

"They jus going back and forth cause they jus killed one of their boys tha other day."

"Shit jus so sad, don't make no damn sense; now two mothers gotta bury their sons."

"They said Dame mom is sickly."

"AIDS?"

"No, jus that she's real sick."

"Damn, I hope this don't drive her to her grave. I'm glad I don't got no brothers."

"Me too sis."

"He's jus not having a good day at all."

"What else happened?"

"Sanchez ain't tell you?"

"Unh I haven't spoken to him since this morning." I gave her the quick version of the story.

"Damn, but I knew it was only a matter of time before that shit happened."

"I was surprised they let it go this long." I signaled for Kelly to give us two more shots."

"Here you go ladies."

"Thanks Kelly."

"No problem."

Claire put some money in the Jukebox to soften the dim mood. When Futures 'March Madness' came on everybody got hype."

"I see a few ballers in here tonight."

"Yeah, too bad I'm spoken for."

"I know that's right," Claire said hi-fiving Tessa.

"Awe Shit," Tessa said looking towards the door.

Claire turned to see what she was talking bout.

Bump walked in without a care in the world he was a known Stick Up Kid. Who at one point probably robbed everybody in here. All eyes were on him as he slid to the bar.

"Wonder where he's been? Haven't seen him or heard his name mentioned in a while."

"I heard he was down Maryland doin his thing."

"Damn down there robbing niggaz now?"

"No, down there eating."

"Bitch who was crazy enough to put him on?"

"Cannon."

"Stop lying."

"I'm dead serious."

"Well he damn sure iced out."

Bump felt all the eyes on him and he loved it because he knew they all feared him. Only if they knew he been stopped jacking niggaz and was now getting major money in Maryland, thanks to his cuz.

Cannon and Sanchez walked in without a care in the world. King really felt uncomfortable now if Bump wasn't enough now these two, but he wasn't about to leave. When Bump had robbed him, he made King strip butt naked and beat him what a broomstick. Bump raised his hand for Cannon and Sanchez to come over.

"They don't even see us."

"I know but they will," Tessa said with a smile.

"What's up Cuz?"

"UAlready Cuz."

"What it do Sanchez? UAlready money is tha motive."

"Don't I know it."

"I see everybody out there eyes on you."

"Yeah, I ain't worried bout these niggaz, I jus came to handle my bizness."

"I put them in ya stash box."

"Did you get tha spread to?"

"Yeah."

"I see Tessa and Claire watching y'all."

Both Sanchez and Cannon looked up. Cannon took his hat off and tipped it to them. Tessa blew him a kiss which he caught and put it on his cheek.

"You two are too much," Claire said bagging up.

"Hey Kelly, get them another round of whatever they're drinking and then come get our orders please."

"I got you Cannon." When she gave them their drinks they both mouth the words thank you.

"A'ight what y'all want your usual?"

"Yup, double shots and what you drinkin Cuz?"

"Double shot of Remy straight, matter fact let me get tha whole bottle."

"A'ight be right back."

She came back with our drinks. As I was counting the money Bump put his hand out.

"Put that away Cuz it's on me," he said while pulling out his bankroll and pulling off 5 dubs.

"Keep tha change Kel."

"Thank you."

"Anytime," he said winking at her.

"Cuz Imma probably slide down tomorrow."

"Kool, no problem, I ain't going to be doing shit anyway."

"Kool."

"Yeah, you can see how I run my shit."

"Ha! Ha! Ha!"

"What you laughing at?"

"Did you ever think you would be eating off tha game like this?"

"Hell nah, I was eating off takin niggaz shit, but this is a whole different level."

"Do you worry bout a nigga try'n ta jack you?"

"Fuck no, cause I'll bust my gun in a heartbeat. Fact, if they do so be it, all the muthafuckas I've done stuck."

"I feel that."

"A'ight Cuz, I've been in here too long let me roll."

"A'ight I'll hit you up tomorrow."

"Kool, watch this," he said as the Jukebox stopped.

"A'ight you niggaz know what it is."

When niggaz saw that big ass pistol they started taking off jewelry and emptying pockets.

"Ha! Ha! Ha! That was tha old me," he said walking out the door.

"Yo that nigga crazy," Sanchez said laughing.

Nobody else seemed to think it was funny. Even (I would rephrase this because they are laughing) Tessa and Claire was shaking their head laughing. I looked around at all the tough guys putting their jewelry back on and scooping up their money. The music came back on and everybody went back to what they were doing. Tessa motioned for me to come here so I made my way around to her.

"Hey Babe."

"Hey Sexy. Give me my kiss."

"Your wish is my command," I said planting a big kiss on her lips.

She moaned letting me know she was horny.

"How many of those you had?"

"Too many."

"How about you Claire Bear?"

"Same here."

"Who drove?"

"Her," Tessa said pointing to Claire.

"Yo Bro you got to drive wifey home." Sanchez looked at Claire, he knew that look in her eyes oh so well.

"You know it's on tonight."

"Well let me catch up wit you then. Kelly let me get a bottle of Henny. You might wanna follow suit."

"Nah I'm good, I don't got to be drunk to Dick wifey down good."

"I hear you Babe."

"Facts."

"Neither do I Bro, jus really brings out my inner freak."

"Yes!" Claire said seductively.

"Hey Cannon."

I turned around to see the broad Lisa standing there.

"What's up?"

"You want to buy me a drink?"

"No," Tessa said before I could answer.

"Excuse you but I was talkin to Cannon.

"This is my girl."

"Oh yeah, since when?" I could tell Tessa was about to snap.

"Listen Lisa, not that it matters but I'm good and here go buy yourself a drink?" I said handing her a $20 bill.

"Why the Fuck did you give that bitch anything?" Lisa smiled and walked away but not before brushing up against Sanchez.

"Oh, I see this Bitch bout ta get body slammed," Claire said trying to get up.

"Not tanite Claire."

"I still want to know why you gave that bitch some money."

"Babe jus so she can go bout her bizness."

"Now that bitch thinks she did sum thing."

"If you didn't have so many drinks I would've let you have your way wit her."

"Imma see her again trust and I won't be drunk. Kelly let me get one more, so I can get up out of here."

"I got you and thank you."

"For what Kel?"

"Not beating her ass. Ha! Ha! Ha!"

"You got that," I said.

I took that shot straight to the face. When I stood up I caught a serious head rush.

"Woo take your time."

"I'm kool Baby. Bitch what you laughing at? Don't let this drunkness fool you."

"What ever," Lisa said with a big dumb smile exposing her fucked up teeth, "you better use that 20 and get them fucked up teeth fixed." Lisa stop smiling then.

"You drunk and that's tha only reason I don't beat your ass."

"If that's your excuse then stick to it, jus know if you ever come for me it'll be your last time I promise you that."

"Bitch you keep talkin and Imma jus act like you ain't drunk?"

Lisa said now standing up, "I'm on my way outside."

Cannon had never seen Tessa rumble, but he saw first-hand Lisa's work on a few occasions and he definitely didn't want her to make Tessa look bad. When Tessa saw Lisa stand up she sobered up real fast and so did Claire. Cannon was not about to let them fight over what he thought was dumb and Lisa's pettiness.

As soon as they were outside one of Lisa's girls yelled, "Bust her ass Lisa bet she won't talk that shit no more!"

"Come on Babe, I'm not letting you fight all drunk," Cannon said but the real reason was he knew Lisa could straight up rumble.

"Baby I ain't no fuckin punk."

By now everybody had come out to witness the fight, I'm sure they knew Lisa would win.

"What's up Bitch? You ain't got shit to say now." Tessa was glad this was a night she chose to wear sneakers.

"Bitch you got me chopped."

Cannon was standing in the middle trying to defuse the situation.

"Lisa go head wit that bullshit, she's had too much to drink so clearly you're at an advantage."

"Nah, Cannon ya Bitch had so much mouth in there." Before I could say anything, she reached over Cannon and smacked me.

"Ooooohh Damn! Oh Shit!" Were a couple of things you heard from the spectators.

"Cannon I swear, if you don't move out my Fuckin way," Tessa said with Venom in her voice.

As much as he hated to at this point he had no choice.

"Move Cannon!" Claire yelled pissed as well.

As soon as he did, Tessa caught Lisa with a jab that had her seeing stars. Before Tessa could counter, Lisa's girls stepped in to break it up; really they were try'n to let Lisa get herself together.

"No don't break it up now!" Claire yelled stepping up.

"Move y'all I'm bout to dog this bitch!" Lisa yelled once she got her bearings back.

As soon as they moved Lisa came in swinging which Tessa predicted she would so she was already on the defense ducking and moving. Lisa had managed to get one in and that would be her last.

"Bust her ass Sis!" Claire yelled.

Tessa ducked a hang maker and came up with an uppercut to her chin that clearly rocked her. It was a wrap after that, Tessa hit her with combo after combo then dropped her with a hard body shot.

"I wish you Bitches would," Claire said to her girls when they acted like they wanted to help.

"Daaaamn she look like Ali and down goes Frazier!" somebody yelled.

Tessa stood over Lisa then said, "Bitch like I said, if you come for me it'll be your last time and next time I'll be sober." Cannon was smiling hard like a kid on his birthday.

"Now I need a Fuckin drink."

"Babe, I gotta be real wit you."

"I know, I know, you thought she was gon to beat my ass."

"I've seen her demolish tha roughest broads."

"Oh, you jus thought I was a cute face. Well news flash, my dad told me and Claire our looks would cause us to have many fights."

"Yup, so he taught us how to box," Clare said finishing her sentence.

"He taught y'all well, she only got one."

"Two," Tessa said correcting him, "she stole me."

"Claire you fight like that too?" Sanchez asked.

"Hell no," Tessa said, "she's better than me."

"What?"

"Yup."

"Note to self, never piss her off," Sanchez said. We all laughed at that.

"Baby I need a drink."

"Highway Inn still open, let's get a bottle and then head home."

"I'll hit you in tha morn Bro."

"A'ight and be easy Champ."

"Shut up Sanchez," Tessa said hitting him in the arm.

"OOOOWW! I'm never gon hear tha end of this."

Lisa walked passed as we were getting in the car, but she didn't even look my way.

"Damn Babe, she didn't even look at you."

"If you just got your ass kicked like that, would you?"

"Ha! Ha! Ha! Ha! Well, you won't have to worry about nobody else try'n you after that ass whooping you put on Lisa."

"She can't fight, she jus swings wild and hard."

"Well, she better not come for my wifey."

"Cannon please, you jus knew I was going to get a beat down."

"Guess why they say never judge a book by it's cover."

"Yup, you got that right," she said holding up her fist.

CHAPTER 24

What They Saw with Their Own Eyes

"What's this I hear about you fighting at tha Casbar a few days ago."

"Sum bitch tried me. Why are you grabbing my face Dad?"

"Well, judging by this lil scratch, I'm assuming you bust her ass."

"Yeah, but my body is sore as hell."

"You haven't used those muscles in a while."

"Tell me about it."

"Maybe you should get back in tha gym."

"I jus told Claire that."

"I always see her there."

"I know, she says y'all work out all the time together."

"We do, she has too much energy for me."

"Ha! Ha! Ha!"

"What's so funny?"

"I was thinking about what Sanchez said."

"I don't even want to know."

"Besides that, how have you been?"

"I'm good, I'm thinkin about goin back to work."

"Why?"

"Dad I be bored."

"Maybe you and Cannon need to give me a grandbaby or babies," I had to look at my dad because I couldn't believe he just said that, "I mean, I'm not getting any younger and tomorrow ain't promised for any of us."

"I know, but I don't know if Cannon even wants kids."

"Well, that might be a conversation you two need to have in tha near future.”

“Yeah, probably so.”

“I’ve never seen you this happy wit any of your other boyfriends.”

“Because I wasn’t Dad and for tha record, I’ve only had two other boyfriends. When are you going to get a special sum one in your life?”

“Who says I don’t already?”

“Simple, I haven’t met her.”

“Ha! Ha! Ha! Right you are.”

“Dad if you have sum one that you really like you’ll introduce her to me; that’s one thing I know for sure.”

“Maybe I’ll find her one day, but right now, I don’t have tha time.”

“You know you’re not getting any younger,” I said quoting what he just said to me.

“You are truly my daughter.”

“Are you going to be busy later?”

“Not for you My Love.”

“I wanted to treat you to dinner.”

“To what do I owe this?”

“Nothing.”

“You sure? Last time you treated me, cost me $3,500.”

“Well, not this time, I jus wanted to spend some time wit my dad.”

“What time should I be ready?”

“Maybe about eightish.”

“No problem.”

“Don’t be late.” Tessa looked just like her mother.

“Why are you staring at me like that Dad?”

"You look jus like IDett." Just the mention of my mom's name changed my mood. She passed away when I was 10 while giving birth to my baby brother who also died.

"I'm sorry, I didn't mean to make you sad."

"It's OK, I've been thinkin about her and Lil' Tayo a lot these past few weeks."

"Yeah, not a day goes by that I don't think about tha two of them. It's been 15 years and I still mourn their deaths."

Truth be told, I think that is why my dad refuses to settle down in fear that she will be snatched away like my mom was.

"Well, I'll be back at 8," he said while heading out the door.

Down in Maryland, Cannon couldn't believe it with his own eyes how much money was moving. They sold nowhere near what we did in our vials, yet nobody complained they just spent their money.

"Damn you make it a Hell of a profit if that's what you're doing."

"Wit this product that's all I need, you don't see them complaining."

"Nah, and you got this block jumping."

"Cuz this block generates at least 25 to 30 racks a day easy."

"I believe it."

"Cuz you know you gon have to start selling sum weight."

"Nah, I ain't doin that."

"Hear me out."

"I'm listening."

"I ain't never told you nothing wrong, so trust me on this."

"I'm listening."

"If you keep all tha work for self, that's when tha jealousy and tha envy come in. I know you don't care but you should. When that happens niggaz will do anything to knock you down; anything."

"Cuz, if I do that, I'll be cutting my own throat."

"Know you won't."

"How do you figure that?"

"Simple, you keep your thing raw and step on theirs. Not to tha point its garbage, but to tha point it's good, jus not what you have. So, what you do is turn 4 into 6 and sell that in weight. Keep tha other 6 and move out here."

Bump thought about it and that was still an extra two bricks, so I was winning still.

"I feel you, that's definitely good money."

"Now everybody is happy."

"You got a nice team put together down here too Cuz."

"These niggaz was starving, all they needed was some food on their plate."

"We all need a lil push at times."

"Don't I know it."

"Ralphy!" Bump yelled.

"What up Boss?"

"Hold it down, I'll be back later."

"You know I got this Folk." POP! POP! POP! POP!

On instant Cannon and Bump both pulled their guns out.

"Man, that's Cas over there."

"My fault, y'all niggga selling this .45, had to make sure it worked."

"Come on Cuz let's get up out of here before tha boys swing through."

"Let's swing to tha Waffle House and grab some grub, a nigga starving."

"Kool."

We got to the Waffle House and it was a bit crowded as it always is on a Saturday.

"In or out?" the waitress asked.

"In."

"Follow me please."

"Anything to drink?"

"I'll take a water."

"Sprite for me."

"I'll be right back."

"Hey Ma."

"Shante."

"Huh?"

"My name is Shante."

"Oh, I'm sorry, but you can take my order, I know what I want."

"Me too."

"Let me guess, Chicken and Waffles."

"How'd you know?"

"Assumption."

"Well, very good one."

"A'ight, I'll be back wit your drinks."

"Thanks Ma, I mean Shante."

"Jus doin my job." She was right back with our drinks.

"Thanks, jus doin my job."

"And you do it well," Bump said obviously flirting.

Shante started smiling as she walked away.

"Yeah, I got her lil cute ass."

"Right Cuz."

When Shante came back with our food Bump asked her if he could borrow her pen. When she gave it to him he wrote something down on a napkin and then slid it to Shante along with her pen back.

"It's up to you if you choose to use it and I won't hold it against you if you don't."

"I'll take that into consideration."

"That's all I ask."

"Cute," she said and then walked away.

"If everything goes right I'll probably be grabbing more."

"No problem, I can cover any order."

"So, you got that unlimited supply; is what you telling me?"

"Yup, sum thing like that Cuz."

"Solid, that's what I love to hear."

"They got a Meek Mill's concert coming up in two weeks you try'n to Fuck wit it?" Bump asked.

"Yeah, me, Sanchez, Tessa, and Claire supposed to be Fuckin wit it."

"Kool, cause this shorty asked me to go wit her."

"Asked you to go or asked you to pay her way?"

"Ha! Ha! Ha! Nah Cuz, this is on her dime, she got paper."

"She must got a job at tha bank?"

"Nah, she's a realtor wit her own firm."

"Oh, she got real money."

"Yes Sir."

"Where you meet her at?"

"Her office."

"Damn, that's what's up."

"Yeah, I was try'n to purchase a house and sum body referred me to her office."

"How old is she?"

"31-32, I think."

"Wow and she young, you better wife her up Cuz. You don't find them like that no more."

"She ain't even got no kids."

"Daaamn, that's rare in this day and age."

"Who you telling."

We finished up, left a nice tip, and then headed back to the hood. When we pulled up there were even more people out milling around.

"Cuz if I was you I would up tha size of my vials."

"Huh why?"

"For me it's always about tha quick-flip. If I spend 50k and I only make 60k, but I did it in 2 days, that's a 10k profit. How I'm gon Fuckin complain."

"I see what you're sayin." I could tell Bump was drinking it all up.

"Imma give it a try jus see how it goes."

"I bet you dump your work faster."

"Imma open another block across town."

"A'ight, I'm bout to head back home, jus hit me up when you ready?"

"UAlready Cuz."

"Oh yeah, Cannon."

"What up Cuz?"

"Thanks," he said giving me a big hug.

"Come on we've family; Imma always have ya back, you know that."

"Yeah, even when I was on my bullshit, you never switched up on me."

"Of course not, I might not have agreed to some shit, but I still had ya back."

"True, that's why I never got at none of ya folks."

"Be safe and hit me up?"

"For sure."

CHAPTER 25

Dumb Ass Niggaz

"There that niggga go right there."

"Chill, let's follow him and see where he goes."

Preme saw them before they seen him; he had his hands on his nina ready to squeeze if need be. When he realized they were more than likely going to just follow him he decided to have a little fun with them.

"King, do you think he spotted us?"

"Nah, I'm going to jus stay a few feet back. Once we see where he goes we can come back later and strike."

Preme stopped in front of this run-down apartment building and then parked. Before he got out he looked into his rear-view to make sure they were still behind him. Once he saw them parking he smiled and then got out. King and Strap watched as Preme got out with a bag and looked around.

"Oh, this must be their stash spot."

Preme made sure to grab the duffle bag with his dirty clothes in it just to throw them off. He trotted up the steps to the building, stopping to open up the middle mailbox.

"Dumb ass niggaz," he thought knowing they will come back to check the mailbox to see which apartment that he went into.

Even though the apartment was vacant he still had the key that he didn't turn in. He just hoped they hadn't changed the locks yet. When he put the key in and it turned he had to laugh out loud to himself. He walked up the steps and then hit the lights.

"It's tha 2nd floor King," said more to himself not Strap.

"Come on let's roll."

Preme peeped out the window just as they were cruising by.

"Dumb ass niggaz."

He would have the ultimate surprise waiting on them when they came back. He headed back down the steps and out the door. Float was proud of himself, he had pumped life back into a block that was once dead.

"Damn Babe, you got this block jumpin and in jus three weeks."

"Yeah, this is jus tha start of it."

He had stopped sniffing heroin but picked up another habit of popping perks and drinking Lean (promethazine). Mayla had really started liking Float. At first, it was just sex, but over the past few months she was falling in love with him and fast.

"Float, why are you staring at me like that?"

"Because you are so beautiful."

That she was, 5'5", caramel skin tone, hazel eyes, shoulder length hair, and an ass that any stripper would definitely love to have. She was by far the prettiest female I've had and trust what I say, I've had some pretty bad females in my life.

"Stop, now you got me blushing."

"It's tha truth Baby."

Mayla put her arms around his neck, stood on her tippy toes, and pushed her tongue in his mouth. Float usually kept his feelings in check, but for some reason he could not do that with Mayla.

"Do you know I'm starting to have really strong feelings for you," he said.

"Strong feelings, uh oh," Mayla said joking.

"What does un oh mean?"

"It was jus a joke."

"Oh really?"

"Yes really, but it's funny that you mentioned that cause I feel tha same way."

"I know it's only been four months, but it jus seems a lot longer."

"I really can't explain it."

"Me either, but I'm willing to see where it goes."

"Me too."

"So, does this mean you're my man now and not jus a Fuck buddy."

"Ha! Ha! Ha! Damm, is that what I was?"

"Well, it's what I was right?"

"I don't know, and I honestly didn't, even though she had a nigga turned out. But I won't tell her, that may go to her head."

"Well Mister, how bout we take this to tha bedroom and make it official."

I watched as she turned to head up the stairs. Just watching her ass jiggle when she moved gave me an instant erection.

When she got to the top of the steps she turned around and asked, "Are you jus going to stand there?"

"Nope, on my way now."

By the time I got to the bedroom Mayla was already ass naked spread eagle on the bed with two fingers massaging her clit.

"Damn you move fast."

"You jus come finish tha job."

"Yes Ma'am."

About six orgasms and two hours later, we both laid there satisfied and exhausted. Like all females, it took some time to get used to, but now Mayla handled this pipe like a sure pro.

"Baby, I know comin up you didn't get a lot of ass."

"Huh?"

"Not like that, what I mean is the size of that thing probably scares them off." I laughed but she was right, it was a gift and a curse.

"Shit, you damn near scared me off had I not been drunk." We both started laughing.

"Let's jump in tha shower." After showering and getting dressed, we both went downstairs.

"Baby, I have to run to tha bookstore Uncle wants me to send him a few books."

"Is he into urban novels?"

"Yup, that's all he really reads."

"Well, make sure you grab him 'Who Can You Trust'."

"He asked for that book by Jerz, I think his name is."

"Yeah, that's who wrote it."

"I read his other book, it was good."

"Yeah, he nice, he's from down my way."

"Oh, so you know him?"

"Unh hun he good folks, can't say nothing bad about him."

"Well, I'll make sure I grab it. I'm about to hit tha highway, I'll be back up later."

"A'ight make sure you come back. If not, then call and let me know.

"Kool, I got you Ma." She gave me that look she hate it when I called her Ma.

"I'm sorry Mayla."

"It's a habit that has to be broken, but don't worry I will help you to break it."

"Thank you."

"You're welcome."

After about 45 minutes, I finally made it to Wilmington thanks to all the traffic.

"Yo, what up Float, where you been hiding at?"

"Hiding, nah Nigga, I jus been chillin try'n to stack and stay out tha way."

"I definitely feel you on that."

"Be easy, I'm bout to hit tha barbershop to get my shit cut."

"A'ight."

When Float got to tha shop King and Strap were there.

"Playa, Playa."

"Hey-hey now."

"What's good on ya end?"

"UAlready, need to see you."

"That's what's up."

"Oh, shit there she go." Before we could ask who Strap was already outside.

"What's up Summer?"

"Hey," she said rather flat.

"Damn, like that?"

"Strap, I told you I'm good, I got a man."

"You keep sayin that, but I never see you wit him."

"Well, that's not my problem."

"I don't think you do."

"Why do I need to lie?"

"I don't know, you tell me."

"Listen, if I didn't want to holler I would just say that, not lie about having a man."

"What's his name?"

"Does it matter?"

"I might know him."

"I'm pretty sure you do, who doesn't."

"So, who is this mystery man?"

"Spanish Jose."

"From tha hilltop?"

"Yeah."

"Damn, Summer, I thought you like bosses."

"What's that supposed to mean Strap?"

"I jus thought you like bosses that's all."

"He is a boss."

"Ha! Ha! Ha! Well, when you get tired of fuckin that manager come holler at tha owner," I said while goin back in the barbershop.

"Nigga, how you a boss and you work for King?" Everybody in the shop looked at Strap expecting him to snap.

"Ha! Ha! Ha! You don't even believe that."

"I was gon let you top me off, but you jus blew that," while getting back in her car she said, "broke ass nigga I wouldn't even let you smell my panties."

A few niggaz in the shop found that funny, but Strap didn't.

"You muthafuckas think that was funny?" Nobody responded.

"Jus what the fuck I thought."

"Come on Strap the barber called out trying to diffuse tha situation." Strap jus stood there.

"Fuck it, Cal he don't want to go."

"I'll go, I got shit to do," Float said.

"Nah, niggga you better wait ya turn."

"Well, sit your simple ass in tha chair."

King also wanted to laugh, but he knew how Strap was, so he'd wait until it was just them and fuck with him. Once we were all done we met up at the stash spot.

"This is for what I owe you plus an extra one."

"You must got it jumpin up there."

"Almost."

"You definitely puttin in tha time."

"Me and Mayla really feeling each other."

"I see."

"How so?"

"You no longer refer to her as Ma or Shorty."

"She hates when I call her that."

"Nigga you sound pussy whipped to me."

"She got me speeding in tha fast lane tryin ta get back ta her love."

"Yo, what Mayla?"

"Hey, do you want me to cook or order sum thing?"

"What you cooking?"

"Steak, shrimp, a bake potatoe, and salad."

"Damn yeah, go head in cook."

"A'ight."

"I'll be up in bout 2 hours."

"Oh, OK, wasn't expecting you til much later."

"Nah, a few hours tops."

"OK and you know what's for dessert."

"I'm hoping Cherry Pie."

"And you know it," she said before ending the call.

"Yeah, Strap this nigga definitely whipped."

"Man fuck y'all, she jus a real one."

"She gon bust it for a real one."

"A'ight Quilly."

"Here nigga, take this shit so you can be on ya way to wifey."

"Y'all straight down here?"

"Yeah, we good bout to deal wit a few situations, but ain't shit we can't handle."

"You sure?"

"Positive."

"Kool, I'm only 20 minutes away and I got some young boys that's definitely wit tha shits."

"Right, I'll hit you in a few days."

CHAPTER 26

Last Stop, Claymont

"You sure this tha house?"

"Yeah, this tha address he gave me."

"Come on then, let's get this over wit."

"He said what ever we get it's ours."

"That's even better."

Preme, Dink, and Jason knew it would only be a matter of time before they sent somebody. They all screwed on the silencers and pulled their masks over their faces. SSPPT! SSPPT! SSPPT! SSPPT! SSPPT! SSPPT!

Before they even knew what hit them they all were laying on the porch, steps, and the lawn motionless. Without saying a word, Preme, Dink, and Jason walked off into the night as if nothing had ever happened.

"How did you know they would show up tanite."

"I didn't, I was jus hoping."

"Too bad it wasn't King, Strap, and Float laying there."

"Them nigga bitches they ain't really war ready."

"Ever since they had started copping off Cannon they saw a major increase in their money."

"I think we need to end this before it gets started."

"I was thinkin tha same shit and we have a big advantage."

"What's that?"

"We know where their stash cribs at."

"They probably switched up."

"I highly doubt it, but we definitely have to find out tanite."

One hour later, they pulled up to the first of three locations they intended to hit tanite.

"Swing tha block, make sure we good."

"Everything looked kool."

"Park on tha other block, we gon cut through tha alley and go from tha back."

"They got spot cameras inside so, y'all stay out here while I go inside. Because if they look at tha cameras and see jus one person they won't suspect us."

"Man fuck them niggaz."

"Yeah, we gon kill them anyway."

"Yeah, but not now, we going to take everything they have first."

Dink picked the lock, pulled his mask down, then went in. After being in the house for what seemed like forever, Dink came out with a duffle bag slung over his shoulder.

"Lock tha door back Bro."

After throwing the bag in the trunk they pulled off without a care in the world.

"I doubt we get much out of the other two cause that was the main one, but we want to hit them anyway."

"You damn right we are."

"Pull over right here Jason."

"Which one of y'all wanna go in?"

"I got it."

"This is only a one bedroom so ain't to many spots to check."

Jason slid from behind the wheel and onto the porch. Within a second, he was in; and the funny thing is, he was out just as fast with a grocery bag in his hand. Pop the trunk he threw it inside, then slid back behind the wheel.

"Damn that was fast."

"Wasn't shit in there but this."

"Kool, last stop Claymont."

"It's a good thing King took you to all his spots."

"He didn't, I followed him and did homework jus in case sum thing like this would happen."

"How did you know bout them cameras?"

"There's one in tha front of tha house, so I knew it was one or two more inside."

"You sum thing else Bro?"

When we got to the house in Claymont there were a few people standing around.

"Swing tha block."

"Damn, we might have to let this one slide Preme," said but already knowing the answer.

"Nah, we gon park and wait, unless y'all gotta be somewhere more important."

"Nah, we wait then."

After about an hour, everybody had said their goodbyes and went their separate ways.

"Come on let's go."

"Y'all go head," Jason said, "I'm goin stay here jus in case I have to put sum body to sleep."

"OK, we'll be in and out." In and out, they were both carrying a bag.

"We out, let's head to tha crib see what we got."

After tallying everything up they ended up with a little over 300k and 4 kilos of the same work Cannon had. Dink wondered how they got their hands on that, he would surely holla at Cannon.

The next day, on the block Dink was talking to Cannon.

"Gotta question for you?"

"I'm listening."

"Did any of ya spots get ran up in and not by tha boys?"

"Nah, why you ask me that?"

"Long story short, we hit all King's spots last night; he had 4 kilos of your work."

"Yeah, he went through his cousin and hollered at Dae-Dae."

"Oh OK, but you said you hit his spots?"

"Yeah, they sent three niggaz to hit a spot they thought we had."

"They made front page."

"Oh shit! I did see that on Delaware online this morning."

"I figured I'd rob them then kill them."

"So, y'all should be straight."

"Nigga only had a lil over 300k and 4 kilos."

"Damn, between all spots?"

"Yeah."

"Shit, I thought he was worth more myself."

"He probably got a nice chunk where he lay his head at."

"I hope so or he's ass out."

"Fuck him and I don't play like that, but he was willing to let y'all kill us."

"Then sent three wild reckless niggaz where you thought we stayed."

"Some niggaz jus don't have no loyalty."

"Dink, I always say wit out loyalty there's no trust."

"You're absolutely right too."

"I wish I could see tha look on his face when he realizes he's been got. Ha! Ha! Ha!"

"WHAT THA FUCK! Let me hit Strap!"

"WHAT THA HELL! Damn, let me call King."

"Yo Bro."

"Yo."

"Did you move that paper out of tha spot on Bancroft?"

"Nah."

"Did you move that work from Claymont?"

"Nah, meet me at tha other spot." They both pulled up at the same time. When they got inside they searched but came up empty.

"Let's look at tha tape."

Watching the tape, they knew they had been got, but who was this guy? King couldn't believe it, besides the 50k he had at his house and the 56k that Float owed him he was damn near broke; he felt like crying. Strap had a little over 9k to his name; so, all in all, Summer was right, he was broke.

"Yo, I don't fuckin believe this shit; sum body is going to die."

"You think Los will throw us 10 to get back?"

"I doubt it, but I have enough to get 4."

When Strap didn't say shit King said, "Don't tell me you ain't been fuckin saving no money Bro."

"Man, that shit was coming in so fast I was blowing through it and honestly, I jus started back stackin." King just sat there really pissed.

"FUCK!" He yelled so loud that the neighbors probably heard.

"We gon have to hit tha streets hard for a few weeks. I might have to grab 3 from Gotti at the 30k. Matter fact, Imma see what Float got."

As if on cue, *"My Niggaz, My Niggaz, My Niggaz."*

"What's up?"

"Imma be ready in a few hours."

"Damn, you jus got that yesterday."

"I know but this shit is booming."

I filled him in what we were dealing with and he let me know that a long with the 56k he could put up another 90k which was love. We could turn that into 9 with no problem. I would give him his 3 that he paid for plus an extra 2, but he would have to pay back 64k which he was kool wit.

"Hit me as soon as you on your way."

"I got you Bro, no problem, give me a least 2 hours."

"Damn, that was right on time, Float is going to put 90k up along wit tha 56k he owes."

"That's what's up," Strap said but King could hear the envy.

"In house job you think?"

"How could it be? Nobody knows about these spots but us."

"That's what I'm sayin." King didn't like what he was saying.

"So, what you sayin Strap?"

"I'm jus sayin we get all 3 spots hit and now not only is Float done wit tha work he jus got yesterday, but he's got 90k to contribute." King thought about it, then shook the thought out of his head.

"I don't think he had anything to do wit it, he's been stacking his bread unlike some people."

"So, what you sayin King?"

"I said it."

"I ain't try'n ta hear that."

"Jus like I'm not try'n ta hear what you spittin about Float."

"I'm jus stating tha obvious."

"Oh, and I'm not?"

"You know what it's obvious, we both need to kool off so, I'll hit you up later."

"Yeah, a'ight."

Strap decided he was going to see for himself jus how this block Float had up North Philly was booming. King picked up a chair and threw it across the room.

"Fuck! Fuck! Fuck! How could this happen?" he kept asking himself over and over again.

He knew in his heart that Float would never cross him like that, they had been friends ever since first grade. Besides, if he was the one, he wouldn't need to holla at me because he would have the 4 bricks of raw. At the end of the day, one of them had been followed, but by who? King knew he would have to grind hard to get back what he lost plus more. He made a promise to himself that he would never feel like he did now ever again.

When Strap pulled up he couldn't believe his eyes. Float had this block looking like a block party; all the people that were coming and going. He watched for close to 3 hours and he could most definitely see how Float would be done so quick.

As he pulled off, he observed the whole scenery, that's when he saw the two guys on the rooftops holding semi-automatic machine guns. He had to admit, Float definitely had something good going on up here. Strap felt bad about assuming Float had something to do with the break-ins at the stash spots. He would definitely let King know and apologize.

A few hours later, King was meeting up with Gotti to grab 7. Float had come with 120k instead of the original 90k he said. King was gon turn this 7 into 10½ easy. So, Float would get 6 instead of 5 at the same price as before. Once King got with Gotti he hit the Lab, handled his biz, and then hit Float.

"I know you had to do ya thing, I jus hope you didn't put too much."

"Nah Bro, it's still a 10 on tha scale."

"Do you have any idea who might have hit tha spots?"

"Nah."

"Damn."

"Float, I really want to say thanks Bro."

"Come on Bro, I wish I had more to contribute."

"What you gave up was plenty, it allowed me to grab 7, if Gotti wasn't hitting me for 30k we could have did more."

"7?"

"Yeah, ya 120k and my 90k."

"Why Strap ain't give up shit?"

When he didn't respond Float knew the answer. He was doing what I used to do, spending without saving.

"It's kool, he jus gotta stack this round."

King did not have the heart to tell Float, Strap thought it was him after hearing what Float just said.

"I'm bout to jump back on this expressway, I'll be at you as soon as I'm done."

"A'ight Bro and thanks again."

"Ain't bout shit, you been lookin out for me all my life Bro, so it's bout time I'm returning tha favor."

King gave Float a brotherly hug and said, "I love you Bro."

"I love you too Bro."

CHAPTER 27

Somebody Robbed All King's Spots

"Heeeey Sis."

"What's up Claire? I haven't seen or talked to you in a few days."

"That's only because you've been busy wit Sanchez."

"I know right."

"Sis as long as you happy, that's all that matters."

"I am happy, I can see us together for a long time."

"You sure deserve it too. Oh yeah, you know I saw Lisa tha other day."

"Did you, what she say?"

"Not a fuckin thing, she jus stared wit her ugly ass."

"Ha! Ha! Ha! Where you see her at?"

"Red Lobster, I treated Daddy to dinner."

"Damn, no invite?"

"You was already on a movie date."

"How you know?"

"Cannon."

"Figures. What Dad talkin bout?"

"Same shit, we need to give him some grandbabies cause he's not getting no younger. I tell him almost every day at tha gym, we are not ready to be mother's yet. Sis you know what he said?"

"I know. (in my daddy voice) Why are y'all not ready? You both are established and have all tha means to provide for him or her."

"Ha! Ha! Ha! That sounds jus like him."

"I know right. (LOL) Starting Monday, I want to hit tha gym wit you."

"Awwwe shit."

"I'm dead serious, I got to get in shape."

"You look fine to me."

"After that fight, my body was sore as shit."

"Cause you ain't used them parts in a while."

"I know, same shit Daddy said to me."

"We got a good work out plan."

"Y'all ain't gon to work me to death have a bitch fucked, not be able to walk or fuck."

"You stupid."

"No, I'm dead serious." (LOL)

"Damn, Baby I'm sore from tha gym so, I can't give you no pussy tonight."

"I swear you simple, after tha first few days you'll be good though."

"Plus, I want to give this some more umph," I said grabbing my ass.

"Sis, you don't need no more umph, trust me, but I got sum thing that will really help round it out."

Mmmm, Uh, Oh, more round my baby's gon to love that."

"Yes, he will because Sanchez can't get enough of cupping and squeezing this ass."

"Bitch and loves every minute of it."

"Yeeees Bitch, yes loves it."

"I'm definitely getting in tha gym though; plus, I started my yoga classes back up tha other day."

"Damn Sis."

"What? I told you when you started back I wanted to go wit you."

"How long ago was that?"

"I don't remember."

"So, what makes you think I would?"

"I jus got some more of that sour watermelon."

"Well, why isn't it in the air?"

"It's in tha kitchen drawer, roll it up."

"Well God damn, I mean, did you get enough?" Claire asked after opening up tha drawer.

"That shit don't come around often so, I had to get a QP (quarter pound), shit if he had more I would of got more of it."

"I know that's right, you gotta sell ya Sis some of this."

"I got an eighth for you."

"An eighth, damn at least sell me a half."

"Nah, jus give me 250 and weigh out a zip."

"Now that's what I'm talkin bout. Imma owe you 50, only got 200 on me."

"No problem, jus roll sum thing up, I ain't smoked all day."

"Have you heard tha latest gossip."

"No, you know I don't be in to all that."

"Me either, but you know they always in tha salon running erybody's bizness."

"Awe shit, what's going on now?"

"Sum body robbed all King's spots; now, he's supposed to be broke."

"Wow."

"I know right, I told Sanchez they better make sure they shit tight. They done put them damn dogs in them houses."

"Shit, a muthafucka will shoot them."

"Same shit I told him."

"What he say?"

"If they do tha neighbors will hear and call tha police."

"Shit, they'll be long gone by tha time tha police get there."

"He said they'll never find what they came to get. Cannon told me one time that if tha police were to run in any of their spots, they won't even find shit."

"Oh, they on some James Bond 007 shit."

"Ha! Ha! Ha! Damn this shit's gas, I'm high as a plane."

"Me too."

"You feel like going out later?"

"Sure, as long as it's not down here."

"I was thinking up top somewhere, it's Friday so, I know it's a few things going on."

"Imma get on I.G. (Instagram) and check tha boy Willa page he always got shit going on or tha other boy."

"Who, T.J. Get Right?"

"Yeah, that's him."

"They suppose to be having a party next month for that boy Mase that was killed a few years ago."

"Who?"

"His crew."

"Oh, homewreckers cause I was bout to say they don't fuck wit Willa."

"I ain't really know Mase like that, but when I did see him he was always on some kool shit."

"Yeah, that was my boy, he was definitely a real one, always talkin bout duuh dummy."

"Well, let me know when it is, I'll definitely be there."

"They gon need a big ass building because he's gon bring tha whole city out like he did for his funeral."

"I heard about that."

"I've been to a lot of funerals Sis, but I've never seen one like that and that church was big as shit."

"Didn't they take him away in a horse and carriage too?"

"Yup, it was beautiful."

"A'ight enough bout that, a bitch bout to start crying."

"Shit, I almost forgot."

"What?"

"I ordered you one of those bags you wanted."

"Bitch no you didn't."

"Yes, I did, it'll be here in a few days."

"How much I owe you?"

"Nothing it's on me."

"Damn, Cannon has definitely been putting it on you."

"Sis stop, I always make sure you straight."

"You do and vice versa."

"So what time do you wanna leave?"

"Bout 1, no later than 11:30."

"See you later and I'll have that 50 for you."

"Kool, no problem. Lock tha door on ya way out."

After Claire had left I decided to take a shower and get some rest for tonight.

CHAPTER 28

STILL NO WORD?

"Still no word?"

"No Ma. We've killed and tortured everybody he had beef wit."

"A reliable source told me that it was a case of mistaken identity and that tha shooters were from Philly." Trans and Cinco both looked at their mother.

"Are you sure Ma?"

"Have I ever not been," Amelia said staring Cinco straight in his eyes. Cinco knew that look all so well.

"So, are you saying that they were killed by mistake?"

"Yes, but I'm still trying to get tha names and where about of those who were involved in this no matter if it was a mistake or not. But on to other bizness." They both waited even though they knew what was coming.

"I see there has been a declined in carbs sales."

"Yeah, he lost his major player to a Texas supplier."

"Well, maybe if he wasn't so greedy this wouldn't have ever happened."

"He's too damn greedy?"

"I believe tha Texas plug is a 15k a brick."

"It must be trash at that price."

"I don't know."

"We don't even know who he was dealing wit to even see tha quality of tha work. Pete has been a nice pick up though."

"What price do you charge him?"

"25k."

"Drop it 21k, see if that really picks it up for him."

"A'ight, I'll call him after this since I'm supposed to meet him tonight."

Cinco hit Pete's phone, after the 3rd ring he picked up.

"Cinco my Man."

"What up Pete?"

"Same shit different smell."

"I got some good news for you."

"Oh yeah, well, let a niggga hear it."

"Imma drop 4 points for you so that you have plenty of room to wiggle wit."

"Awe shit, now that's what I'm talking bout."

"I knew you like that."

"Of course, I'll hit you back wit my new amount in about 30 minutes."

"No problem."

Pete couldn't believe it, he could definitely make some noise now and maybe even compete with King and Cannon. He would get 15 instead of his normal 10 to start out. He would also have to put his plan on hold for a lil longer now while he really got his paper up.

Cinco was kool with the additional 5 simply because he knew the 5 would eventually turn into 10 or 20 extra. They would meet up at 7 pm at the usual spot. Cinco was starting to get comfortable with meeting Pete, so he was bringing less people when he did come. Before leaving Pete let him know he probably be back at him in a few days tops. Cinco liked the sound of that. At first, Cinco didn't like the idea of having to deal with the street hustlers, that was Miguel job, but he was starting to like it for some strange reason it gave him a rush.

CHAPTER 29

I'm Cumming Again!

It had been a little over a week and still no word on who hit King's spots. King thought by offering $10,000 that somebody would have come forward with the information, but as of yet, not a word have been spoken. Since he was doing all the leg work he had really seen a profit.

"Strap we might have to do this all tha time if tha profit is this good."

Strap could not front, it was definitely worth the profit and at this rate he would have his stash up in no time. Strap made a promise to himself that he would never ever be in that position again and he meant it.

"I don't know if I told you this or not, but Float got that block up there doin crazy numbers."

"I can tell he hit me earlier, said he'd be ready again by 7 pm."

"If I wasn't sitting out there and seeing it wit my own eyes I would have never even believed it."

"I'm telling you that block gotta be doin at least 30k a day."

"Shit it's probably more than that, tha nigggga running through 6 kilos every 3-4 days."

"I'm proud of him."

"Me too, that's why I didn't intrude; it's his time to step out of tha shadows."

"I was surprised cause he's always wanted to play tha back."

"Well, he lettin Mayla brother control tha tempo."

"Yeah, but they know he's calling tha shots."

"You think they will try any funny shit?"

"I doubt it and if they do Float is war ready."

"Nigga, I'll air that whole block out, no questions asked."

"Facts."

"I'm bout to go take my people's lunch."

"Damn, you and shorty still kickin it? That's some good shit she got to keep you around this long." (LOL)

"You crazy, told you she got her own paper, besides she don't be pressing or stressing a nigga like tha rest of these broads."

"Yeah, cause her people's definitely putting tha full court press on a niggga right now." (LOL)

"I'm bout to pick Lee-Lee up and spend sum quality time wit her I've been neglecting my baby these past few weeks."

"Tell her uncle King says he loves her and I'll see you later."

"A'ight, yo so what's up wit Banita?"

"Bro that shit's over." Strap just left it like that.

"Picking up an order for King."

"$21.85."

"Here you go."

"Thank you, have a good day."

"You too."

10 minutes later, King was pulling up to Jazzman's office.

"Hello, may I help you?"

"Yes, I'm here to see Jazzman."

"Hold on" she pushed a button and then said, "there's a gentleman here to see you."

"Send him back Kandis."

"OK...Sir straight back,"

"Thanks."

"You're welcome."

"Hello there."

"Hey, I didn't think you were comin."

"It's 1:20 pm, you said you take lunch at 1:30."

"I know but I thought you would call to say you couldn't make it."

"Haven't I proved that I don't lie?"

"Yeah, kinda sort of."

"What's that suppose to mean?"

"Jus a joke."

"Oh well, I got you a grilled chicken salad wit a nice spring water."

"That's crazy, I've been craving a salad."

"I jus hope it's good. I got it from Lucy's."

"Who?"

"Lucy's on Market Street."

"I don't know where that is."

"It's over by McDonalds."

"Oh, that spot across from Rite Aid?"

"Yeah."

"I never ate from there before."

"Well, you should like it if you like a good salad," I said taking it out of the bag.

She looked at it and then said, "It even has eggs. Yeah, they look like they know what they doin."

"I hope you like Blue Cheese and Italian dressing?"

"Boy you on point today, you definitely earning sum kool points."

"Now that's what I like to hear." We sat in her office and talked while we ate lunch.

"I must admit this salad is off tha hook."

"I'm glad you like it, next time I want to turn you on to sum thing else."

"What?"

"You'll see."

"What are you doing later?"

"I don't know."

"Well, if you're not too busy maybe you can stop by for dinner."

"What time do I need to be there?"

"8:30-9."

"I'll be there. Do you need me to bring anything?"

"Yeah, condoms."

This caught King off guard causing him to choke on his water. Jazzman jumped up to aid him.

"You OK?"

"Yeah, you caught me off-guard wit that."

"I know, and I was jus joking," she said smiling.

"*I figured that,*" King thought to himself.

They've been talkin for a minute now and he couldn't even begin to tell you what her panties look like. Truth is he had never even tried to get in her panties he was waiting on her to make the first move.

"*If he only knew I wasn't really jokin I respect he didn't try to Fuck me yet, but damn a bitch was ready for tha real deal,*" she said to herself. Jazzman hadn't had anything but plastic in her for the past two years. King was the first man she had even talked to since her last relationship two years ago. She thought back on that day when she found out her then boyfriend had been living a double life. Jazzman always wondered why he never stayed the night and when he did he'd always leave at 1 am like clockwork.

One day or should I say morning, I decided to follow him to see if in fact he was going to work like he claimed. He had pulled into a nice development and then pulled up to a nice home. I took a mental note of that address so that I could come back later that day.

I called Kandis and let her know I would be in after 1 pm and to reschedule any appointments before then. I pulled up just as Justin was leaving. I started to block him in, but I thought of a better idea. I set there for a second just to make sure he didn't double back. Once I was sure he wasn't, I got out and walked up to the door. Just as I was about to knock the door opened.

"Oh, I'm sorry, did I catch you at a bad time?"

"I was on my way to tha grocery store, how may I help you?"

"I jus wanted to ask you a few questions about Justin."

"Who?"

"Justin."

"I'm sorry but I don't know any Justin."

I went to grab my phone out my pocket book but then remembered I don't have any pictures of him. He had deleted them all by mistake, so he claimed.

"That guy that jus left."

"Oh, that was my husband Devon."

As soon as the word husband left her mouth I fainted. When I came to I was sitting in her living room staring at the many pictures of her, Justin, and

I'm assuming their children.

"Are you OK?"

"I think so. You said Justin is your husband?"

"Devon is my husband of 21 years."

"Well Mrs…"

"Tara, call me Tara."

"Tara I'm sorry to inform you but I have been in a relationship wit Justin, I mean Devon for tha past 2 years."

"Are you sure we're talkin about tha same man?"

Jazzman had just remember the picture she had took a few nights ago of Devon in her bed sleep with his mouth wide open. I turned my phone so that she could see the picture. Tara instantly started to cry. After I told her the whole story I apologize to her.

"Jazzman you have nothing to be sorry about, for you knew nothing about me as I knew nothing about you." As the conversation was ending the front door came open.

"Mommy, Mommy," the twin boys said running into Tara's arms.

When Devon walked through the door his eyes popped open and his mouth dropped.

"Close your mouth Justin," Tara said with venom in her voice.

"Jah'ceer and Nah'ceer go play in your room so we can talk."

"Ok but who is she Mommy? She's pretty," Jah'ceer said.

Jasmine smiled and then said thank you. She knew he would grow up to be a ladies man and a charmer.

Once the kids were gone Tara said, "Care to explain."

Devon just sat there in silence. Even though Jazz was clearly hurt she felt more sorry for Tara.

"No disrespect to you Tara, but I don't want to hear it. You told me all I needed to know so, if your excuse me I'll let myself out."

"Jazzman, Jazzman."

"Huh."

"You were in la-la land," King said as he stood up to leave.

"I'm sorry."

"It's OK, I'll see you later tonight."

"A'ight bring a bottle of Remy."

"No problem," I said and then kissed her on the forehead.

Jazz was definitely wifey material and I could tell that she had been really hurt before. After King left Kandis came in.

"Jazz he is sexy as shit."

"Yeah, he's kinda cute."

"Kinda."

"I know right."

"Does he have a brother?"

"I don't know."

"Girl you better not let him get away."

"I'm thinkin about giving him sum of this good good."

"Jazz you mean to tell me you haven't gave him tha punany yet?"

"Nope."

"He's a definite keeper."

"He hasn't even tried to get in my panties."

"You sound like you disappointed."

"I am, it's been two years."

"Well, it's obvious he's not going to try anything."

"I know, that's why I invited him to dinner tanite."

"Ooooh it's going down."

"I sure hope so, a bitch tired of plastic and batteries."

"Ha! Ha! Ha!"

"Seriously."

"I feel you, I was like that during my 6-month drought."

"No not Ms I need it 4-5 times a week."

Later that evening Jazz was in the kitchen almost done when the doorbell rang. When I opened the door, King was standing there with a bottle of Remy in one hand and roses and the other.

"Are you goin to invite me in?"

"Oh, I'm sorry, come in. Let me get a vase to put those in."

"You got it smelling good in here Babe I mean Jazz." Jazz had to smile when she heard King call her babe.

"A nigga can get used to this."

"What?"

"A home cooked meal."

"I'm pretty sure one of your other broads cook for you all the time." King found it cute how she was fishing again.

"Listen Jazz, I told you I don't have a girl or any other broads."

"Why don't I believe that?"

"I don't know." She came out with two plates and sat them on the table.

"Would you like juice, water, or soda?"

"Nah, I'll take some Remy on ice though."

"Kool." We both sat down to eat so I started the convo back up.

"Like I was saying Jazz, I was in a relationship, but she wasn't."

"Meaning?"

"I was wit her being faithful, but she wasn't."

"Wow. Sounds like my last relationship."

"Really."

"Yeah, I was wit him for two years, but he was married."

"Married?"

"Yes."

She gave me the quick version of the story. I knew she been hurt but not of this magnitude.

"Damn I guess we both been played before."

"Yup, but never again."

"Cheers to that," I said raising my glass.

"Cheers." I had a better understanding of King now.

"As far as tha other females it's nothing or it was nothing."

"Was?"

"Yeah, since we talking I haven't been wit any of them."

I saw the way she looked at me, so I showed her my empty class, I saw that look and yes, I'm saying I haven't been intimate in the past few months.

"Wow, you must really like me."

"You think so."

At that point my mind was made up King would definitely be up in me tanite. I poured us both another drink, I had to admit the effects of the Remy had a bitch warm on the inside.

"I don't want to keep you if you have sum thing to do or sum where to be."

"Nah, I'm good."

"Well, kick back, relax Imma jump in tha shower and get comfortable, if that's OK wit you?"

"Do you, I ain't going nowhere."

I downed the rest of my Remy, poured another glass, and headed up the steps to the shower.

Damn just watching her walk up the steps gave me an instant erection, but I already knew how this night would end the same as the others as we snuggled on the couch sleep. After what seems like forever Jazz came back down looking like a goddess with her white nightgown on.

"Why you looking at me like that?"

"You are simply beautiful."

"Thank you," she said clearly blushing, "would you like a refill?"

"Please." We drank till the bottle was empty and then talked.

"Wow, I didn't know that we had so much in common King."

"You'd be surprised." She moved closer and put her head on my chest.

"Damn, I'm so horny please touch on me," I thought to myself but knowing he probably wouldn't.

"Are you staying tha night?"

"I normally do."

"Well, let's sleep in tha bed this time."

I didn't get excited because I still wouldn't try anything. When we got to the bedroom smooth sounds of Keith Sweat was playing.

"I'm sorry, I was listening to that while I was in tha tub."

"No, you can leave it on, that's my boy." Jazz pulled off her nightgown revealing her matching bra and panties.

"I hope you don't mind, but I don't sleep in my gown."

"I'm Kool."

"Truth be told, I normally sleep nude."

"Don't let me stop you."

She smiled and got under the covers. When I got up she asked if I was leaving.

"I was going to tha bathroom if that's OK wit you?"

"Ha! Ha! Ha! Boy go head." While he was in the bathroom I slid off my panties and bra.

"What you doing?"

"Getting in bed."

"Ha! Ha! Ha! Boy if you don't take your clothes off, I know you don't go to bed at home like that."

"Nah, I normally sleep nude," I said testing the waters.

"Don't let me stop you," I came back with to see if he would really get naked.

To my surprise he did and wheeeew he was packing, my dildo ain't have shit on him. When I got in bed and she scooted back so that we were spooning I was shocked that she was also naked. I don't know if it was her fat ass or the Remy, but my shit started growing.

"Well I see sum body is excited," she said then started to grind her soft ass on me.

At that moment, for me it was more than enough of the cat and mouse game. I put my hands on her breasts and gently massaged her nipples bringing them to life. "Aaagghh," was the sound that escaped my mouth it had been so long since I've been touched on like this. I turned to face him without saying a word, I put my tongue in his mouth. Before I knew what was going on he put me on my back while his tongue explored my body.

"Ooooohh that feels SOOO good."

As soon as he put his tongue on my box, "Oh My Fuckin God! Oooohh Shiiit! Aaagghh Yes Baby!"

I used my hands to guide him to the spot I wanted and needed him to be. When his tongue hit my clitoris, it was over; I started shaking and had an orgasm.

"Oh My God! I'm Cumming! Shit! Fuck!" Damn he did this thing with his tongue that made me cum again.

"Kiiiing! I'm Cumming Again! Oh My God What Are You Doin to Me!"

At this point, I just wanted to feel him inside of me. I pulled him up so that he could slide in me and as soon as he put the tip in I knew it was going to be a night to remember.

Jazz was tight, so I took my time easing it in until I had all of me inside of her. I couldn't front she felt so good. Next thing I knew she took control and it was over, she did things I never had done. Shit, I almost told her I love her it was so good. *(LOL)* Before we realized it the sun had come up and we were still at it, but no longer fuckin, making love. We both climaxed at the same time.

Not wanting it to be over we just laid there with me inside of her. When it felt like he was going limp, she squeezed her muscles tight around him making him jump back to life.

"I don't think I'm going in today," she said with a smile.

"I jus wanna stay in bed all day wit you."

She looked at me and said, "Don't play cause I'll make it happen."

"Well, make it happen." She picked up her phone.

"Kandis."

"Hey Girl, you going to be late?"

"No, I'm not coming in today and you can take tha day off wit pay," I said and then started grinding my hips.

"Oh, you done got tha real deal last night and it got you fucked up."

"You know it (aaagghh)," I said letting the soft moan escape my mouth.

"Bitch you still gettin it in?"

"Goodbye Kandis."

"Details," she said before hanging up.

"See done do you think you can handle this all day?"

"Sure can."

It was definitely going to be a loooong day. I couldn't front this was the best sex I've had in my life and I'm pretty sure he feels the same way and I didn't even give him everything.

After few more orgasms we both were knocked out, but he was still up in me. (LOL) He said when he woke up he wanted to already be in it and that was fine by me.

CHAPTER 30

Which One's Poppin Tonight?

"Damn you not dressed yet?"

"Bitch that weed knocked my ass straight out."

"Me too but I set my alarm. Ha! Ha! Ha!"

"I should have did that, but I'm almost ready, roll sum thing up."

"Already did before I left tha house."

"Did you roll enough to hold us over?"

"Three."

"Roll up two more." When I got downstairs Claire was just finishing up.

"You ready?"

"Who's driving?"

"It don't matter, you drive up and I'll drive back."

"Where we going?"

"They having sum thing at Roxy's and sum other club I forgot tha name, but it use to be tha old Palmer's."

"Which one's suppose to be poppin tanite?"

"Both tha way it sounds."

"Well, it don't matter."

We rode past the old Palmer's first, it was packed so we headed to Roxy's

"Well, we know which one going to be poppin."

"Let's find a spot to park."

"Jus park in tha casino like we always do."

As soon as we walked up a bouncer was saying it was $30 to cut the line; that was a no brainer. We handed him the 60 and slid right in.

"Hey Ma, won't you let us pay y'all way in."

"We Kool, we got it."

"Oh, ya man gave you enough spending money?"

"Yup," I said making sure he knew I was not available.

"What about you?" he said to Claire?

"Yeah, he even gave me enough to buy a bottle or two."

"Word, that's what's up. He a real nigga, make sure you hold on to him."

"I plan to."

"Well you ladies enjoy your night."

"We will, you do tha same."

"Though I was going to have to cuss them out."

"Any other nigga would've talk shit and still try to spit game."

"All thirsty."

"50."

"Well Damn, who's performing?"

"Pnb Rock."

"Oh, but he still not worth 50," Claire said handing her a crisp Ben Franklin, "no change, that's for both of us."

"Sanchez must've hit you lovely you paying a bitch way."

"I ain't paying ya way that was the 50 I owed you from that good ass watermelon."

"Speaking of did..."

"Yes," she said cutting me off.

As soon as we hit the top of the steps you could smell the different weeds being smoked.

"Damn it's packed, ain't no way all those people getting in here."

"Let's get a booth so we can get a bottle."

"Or two cause I'm not drinking no Brown." We walked over to an open booth, but the bouncer stopped us.

"Is this booth occupied?"

"Nah, but it's 100 for a booth."

I thought he was try'n to scam us till I saw the two guys from downstairs pass off and then got the same color wristband that was on top of their booth.

"I got it Claire." I peeled off five 20's, "we want two bottles too." He looked at us like we just called him gay.

"The bottle girl will be by in a few."

She stopped to get the two dudes order first and then told us she'll be right back. She came back with four bottles for them.

"That's right my nigggaz show them how to do it," the DJ said.

They had two bottles of Remy and two bottles of Bel-Air.

"Hey Ladies, what can I get you?"

"A bottle of Remy and Bombay."

"That's $600."

Me and Claire looked at each other but decided not to respond. We just both dug in our pocketbooks and handed her 6 Franklin's.

"I'll be right back."

"That's 600," Claire said mocking her, "she fucked her tip up."

"Awwe Shit! Tell 'em Ladies, you can pop bottles too," the DJ said seeing the bottle girl bring us two bottles.

We both tipped our bottle to the DJ.

"This one's for all my bottle poppers," he said.

"Run the Check Up and Get It Right Back."

"Heeey and you know we will," Claire sang with the song.

"Let me see ya lighter." As soon as I lit that sour watermelon all eyes were on us.

"Excuse me."

"Yes."

"If you don't mind me askin, what is that you smoking on?"

"Sum sour watermelon."

"That shit smell like sum gas."

"Oh trust, it's most definitely that gas."

"You try'n to sell sum?"

"Nah, sorry Playa."

"Kool, I had to ask."

"I ain't mad at you I would have done tha same too."

"Well, enjoy tha rest of your night."

"We intend to, you do likewise."

By the time Pnb Rock hit the stage we were both feeling good. As soon as he started performing Fleek the chicks went Bezek.

"Hair on Fleek, Nails on Fleek, Make up on Fleek, Shorty on Fleek."

Funny thing is the ones who should be singing along with him ain't. They both looked and were surprised to see our little cousin Sabrina.

"Now who ID did you use to get in?"

"Yours of course," she said holding up Claire's ID.

"No wonder I couldn't find that, you never gave it back."

"Actually, you told me since I was using it so much to jus keep it."

"I did?"

"Yes, you did."

"Must have been one of my drunk nights."

"Well, I won't need it after next year."

Sabrina and Claire could pass for twins only difference is where Claire has gray eyes and a donkey, Sabrina has green eyes and her butt is a little smaller than Claire's.

"Who you up here wit?"

"Need you ask," she said pointing to the dance floor.

"Ha! Ha! Ha! I should've known, that girl is always on tha floor shaking her ass."

"Y'all going to Vanity or Onyx after this?"

"Probably Vanity, Onyx is too ghetto for me."

"YFN Lucci gon be at Vanity."

"Is he?"

"Yeah." I looked at my watch, it was almost 12:30.

"Tessa we bout to roll so we can get there and park in tha lot."

"Come on then."

"Cuz y'all want to finish these bottles off."

"Of course, we do," Keisha said.

"Heey y'all."

"Hey Siya."

"Y'all look stunning as usual."

"So do y'all." They were like a younger us.

"Well, y'all go head so once we get there I know they won't remember anybody using this ID." The bouncer looked.

"They gonna finish tha bottles and be gone." I slid him two 20's and he was kool.

CHAPTER 31

Roxy's

"20 lets me get a spot up front?"

"40."

"No problem."

"Did you call tha owner?"

"Nah, I'm bout to jus see if we can get a booth wit out calling."

"You think Tessa and Claire will be there?"

"YFN Lucci is gon be here and Tessa loves his music, so probably."

"We might as well pay for them a spot in tha booth too." The Bouncer from last time was at the door so he asked if we wanted a booth.

"Yeah, and I also want to pay for two more bands cause our wives will be here if they not already in there."

"No problem, jus give me two racks and I'll have Bunny take you to a booth."

We decided to get a middle booth, so we could see Lucci perform. A few of the chicks remembered us and got excited when they saw us walk through.

"20 for parking Ladies."

"Do you have any more spots up front?"

"Yeah, 40."

"A'ight."

We were already on and that's why we didn't even realize we parked right next to Sanchez's Benz wagon.

"Come on cause that line is about to get long." It didn't take us long to get in.

"Damn it's packed in here."

"You know my boy Lucci was gon to bring 'em out."

"Shit we going to be all damn night trying to get a drink."

"I'm getting a bottle."

"Me too, what you thought."

"Don't look like no more booths available."

"We should've hit Cannon and got tha owners number."

"We ain't got to do that there's the manager."

"Bitch you mean tha owner."

"Oh yeah, come on."

"Hello."

"Hey Ladies, follow me."

I looked at Claire like damn. She just shrugged her shoulders and followed suit. He led us around the bar to the VIP Section it wasn't until we got to the top of the steps until we realized where he was taking us. Sanchez and Cannon had all the strippers around them. We weren't mad, we were at a strip club and they weren't being disrespectful.

"We were starting to think y'all weren't coming."

"And miss my boy Lucci, I think not."

"What I tell you nigga, pay up." Sanchez peeled off 5 Franklin's.

"Don't be betting on me."

"I didn't I bet on both y'all."

"We don't even wanna know." The owner asked if everything was OK.

"Nah, we need four more bottles, 2 and 2 and 20k worth of ones," Cannon said passing him 21k.

He only charged Cannon 250 a bottle cause as he said he's good money.

Sanchez fired up his Dutch and I knew it was gas, but it wasn't fuckin with this watermelon we had.

I lit my shit up and Cannon asked, "Where you get that melon from?"

"Home."

"Damn, I wish I knew you had that."

"It's in tha drawer, I brought a QP of it."

"Damn that's all?"

"That's all he had."

"Y'all got some fire, it's smell like sum sour fireball."

"It is."

"I see y'all got all the bitches."

"Nah, my boy George got them all," he said throwing up a stack of ones.

YFN Lucci is in the building the DJ announced. All the strippers that was wasn't in our section flew over to his section.

"This Rolle Fit My Wrist Like It was Made for It, I Knew My Time was Comin I Had to Wait for It."

The DJ put that on in the club snapped. The bottles started flowing in the section, not to mention he was making it rain ones. After a while he came down, got on the stage, and did a couple of his songs that I knew word for word. Real always recognize real, he tilted his bottle to Cannon and Sanchez in return tilted theirs back.

By 3 am a bitch was good and drunk and ready to go, but not before I ordered sum of that blazing ass shrimp and chicken fingers they serve.

"Baby I'm ready."

"I didn't drive."

"I did, Claire can ride back wit Sanchez."

"Yo Bro you ready?"

"Yeah, I was waitin on my food, but here she go now."

"Imma drive Tessa's truck cause neither of them can drive."

"I know, what would y'all have done if we wasn't here?"

"We wouldn't be this drunk for starters."

"Yeah, we had two bottles a piece so of course we going to be smashed."

"Two?"

"Yeah, we had bottles at Roxy's before we came here."

"Oh y'all was stuntin."

"I wouldn't call it that."

"We were jus doin what we always do."

"Niggaz was definitely hatin y'all." (LOL)

"I know Bro, bottles, ice on, and blowing that good gas." When we got outside I realized we were parked right next to Sanchez.

"Damn Sis, you know we was on, I didn't even realize we parked next to them."

"Ha! Ha! Ha! I'll call you tomorrow Sis."

"A'ight, I love you."

"Love you back."

CHAPTER 32

All-Star Struck & In Love

"Both you niggaz all-star struck and in love," Strap said talking to King and Float.

"Nigga you jus mad," King said pushing him.

"Nah, I'm happy for y'all."

It had been a little over a month and thanks to Gotti and Float they had gotten what they lost and some. Strap even had his paper up not where he wanted it but a lot more than what he started off with.

"Float wants us to come up today, he's having a block party and Neef Buck is suppose to be performing a few of his songs."

"I know, he hit me earlier this morning."

"Imma take Jazzman wit me."

"Nigga you taking sand to tha beach? Cause you know it's gon be sum bad ass broads up there."

"Nigga, my bitch badd wit two D's."

"I never said she wasn't, all I'm sayin is there are going to be a lot of bad bitches up there."

"I'm not worried about them."

"Yeah, you most definitely been hit wit Cupid's arrow directly in tha heart. Ha! Ha! Ha!"

"Nah, Jazz is jus a real one and I'm not gon fuck this up jus for a nut."

"I feel you, I hope I can get me a real one sum time in tha near future."

"What time you goin up top?"

"Once Jazz calls me."

"Oh a'ight, Imma bout to head up so I'll see you when you get there."

"You not riding wit us?"

"Nah, cause knowing me Imma find a broad to get into."

"Kool, I should be up there by 4, 5 at the latest."

"A'ight."

King pulled up to Jazz house and hit the horn. When she came out in her cream YSL sundress King's mouth dropped to the floor.

"Hey Baby," she said getting in and kissing him on the lips.

"You look drop-dead beautiful."

"Thanks," she said blushing, "sorry, I took so long but Ming Lee was backed up today."

"It's kool, I know how much it means to have your feet and nails done."

"Shut up," she said punching my arm. I couldn't take my eyes off her.

"Why you lookin at me like that?"

"I jus told you."

Jazz was 5/6, brown skin, brown eyes, shoulder length hair, and a nice ass that any woman would love to have. But what I really loved was her tattoo that covered her whole right side of her body. It was sum type of Japanese dragon.

"King you always make me feel so special."

"Because you are."

"I keep thinking for sum reason I'm in a dream, you are too good to be true. Ooooww why you pinch me?"

"To show you this is no dream. Strap told me I've been hit in tha heart by Cupid's arrow."

"Ha! Ha! Ha! Leave it up to Strap to say sum shit like that."

"I know right? But I couldn't deny it."

"Well, are we going to jus sit here."

"Oh damn, see you got a nigga fucked up."

"So, ya boy having a block party all way up Philly?"

"Yea, you might as well say he lives up there now wit his shorty."

"Oh, Cupid strikes again."

"Ha! Ha! Ha! Same thing," Strap said.

"Imma stop at tha Highway Inn, grab me a bottle first."

"No problem, I want one of those coolers."

"Let me find out you turnt out on those Jamaica Me Happy."

"It makes me happy as well as horny."

"Well, in that case, I'm gettin you a six pack."

"Sounds good to me."

Since it wasn't crowded I was in and out. I rolled my Dutch then we was out.

"If you look at my life you'll see what I see," Jazz turned up the volume and started to sing with Mary.

"Life can be only what you make it, here's your chance you don't ever have to fake it, say what's on your mind." All I could do was smile because she was giving Mary a run for her money.

When the song went off she looked over at me then said, "Mary is my bitch."

"I had no ideal you could sang."

"Boy you stupid."

"That's how you got to say it when sum body can blow like that."

"Whatever pass tha weed." She took two Puffs and gave it right back.

"You not gon to be wasting my weed."

"I didn't waste it, you know I only need two Puffs and I'm good to go."

"Young lungs."

"I never was much of a smoker, jus wasn't my thing."

"I try to stop but it never seems to work for me."

"You're either not try'n hard enough or you really don't wanna quit."

"Probably C, all of tha above. But I did slow down a whole lot."

"Really?"

"Yeah, shit I was smokin damn near 8 8th's a day."

"Damn, and now?"

"About 3 to 4 at tha most."

"Yeah, you did slow down." I had to park around the corner since they had the block taped off.

"Damn, this Shit live."

"I was about to say that." Jazz put her cream Chanel frames on making her really look good.

"Yo King." I turned to see Float waving me over.

"Come on Babe," I said grabbing her hand since she had a few eyes on her.

"What up Bro?"

"I can't call it."

"Strap ain't make up yet?" Float jus pointed to where Strap was talking to a few females.

"I should've known."

"Hey Mayla."

"Hey King."

"Mayla this is my girl Jazz."

"Hey Jazz, nice to meet you," Mayla said extended her hand.

"Nice to meet you as well."

"Babe we'll be back," Mayla said taking Jazz by the hand pulling her away.

"So, you and Jazz are official now?"

"Yeah, I'll be a fool to let her slip away."

"Same shit I said about Mayla."

"What you two over hear talkin bout, y'all ladies?

"Nah, I was jus telling Float it's live out here."

"Yes, it is and tha ladies is out today."

"What time Neef Buck comin through?"

"Probably bout 7-7:30."

"Roll sum thing up," I said drinking the rest of the Remy I had left.

CHAPTER 33

Strap is a Pussy

"Sanchez what it do Bro?"

"I can't call it, what's up wit you Spanish Jose?"

"Jus try'n get at a dollar."

"I feel you on that."

"I need a lil information if you can help me."

"What kind of information?"

"What's up wit tha boy Strap?"

"What you mean what's up wit him?"

"My girl Summer told me he keeps pushin up on her."

"I'm not surprised."

"It's not even about that because I expect niggaz to do that."

"Right."

"It's that when she told him she's wit me tha nigga started talkin this stop fuckin wit a manager and fuck wit an owner Bullshit."

"Oh word."

"Yeah, Nigga you don't even know me to be speaking on me. If he spit his game and she gave tha nigga tha panties, hey she wasn't never mines."

"I feel you."

"But don't throw dirt on my name and especially when you don't know what I'm doing."

"I don't fuck wit boy no shape or fashion."

"A'ight kool."

"Imma catch up wit him hopefully sooner than later." Spanish Jose already had his mind set as well as made up.

"You be easy out here Sanchez."

"A'ight you do the same." Sanchez watched as Spanish Jose got back in his whip and then pulled off.

"He jus might save me a few bullets."

"What was that about?"

"He needed sum information on Strap."

Dae-Dae looked at me funny and then said, "Information."

"Yeah, evidently Strap been puttin dirt on his name."

"Strap has a death-wish I see."

"Bro that nigga out of here real soon."

A few hours later, on the hilltop the boy Spanish Jose was talking to his boys about his conversation with Sanchez.

"Man, that nigga Strap is a pussy. He got a few bodies on his gun and think he untouchable. Well, Imma show him just how touchable he is. Like Freeway said THINK IT'S A GAME TIL THEM THINGS COME OUT."

Spanish Jose looked at all his boys and then said, "Imma to take care of him," putting emphasis on IMMA, so they knew not to kill him if they happen to run across his path.

Meanwhile, up Philly at the block party Neef was doing his thing on stage. Strap had no idea that he was as they would say a Dead Man Walkin.

"So, I am wit you tanite or what Papi?"

Strap had the choice of choosing between 4 of the baddest females out there. He had no doubt that he would eventually get with them all, but which one would he pick for tonight.

After some thought, he definitely was in the mood for a little Spanish food so he gladly let Marisol know she was most definitely with him tonight. He didn't want to make the other 3 mad so while they were busy watching Neef performed he slid off with Marisol.

"Look at him," Mayla said pointing to Strap.

"He'll never be hit by Cupid," Jazz said causing everybody to laugh.

"That's Strap for you," Float said but still laughing.

"Baby this really turned out to be a nice event."

Despite the all-day drug sales the neighbors loved Float. He made sure they always had the things they needed whether big or small. If they need groceries he got it, if their car needed fixing he handled it. Some of the older neighbors even held the drugs and guns for him. I guess it was their way of showing their gratitude. Even though it was a block party that didn't stop, the money from being made the Fein's even got to get a meal which they were more than willing to take with them.

"I'm bout to head back down this highway my baby done."

"A'ight, I'm bout to go myself, a nigga tired."

Float gave King a brotherly hug and then let him know he would be down to see him tomorrow anyway.

"Kool, you ready Babe?"

"If you are." I put my arm out so she could grab it since she was going to need my help anyway.

"Jazz make sure you call me."

"Don't worry I will."

On the ride back, Jazz turned the music down, so she could talk to me.

"King, I know we've only been messing for a few months, but it feels and seems like longer," I didn't know where this was going so I remained quiet and just listened, "for the past 6 months I looked to see if you would hurt me. The reason being, I didn't want my heart broken again. I don't think I could handle it. You've been nothing but a gentleman. Shit, not many if any men would wait 4 months for sum ass. That alone let me know you were different, not to mention you were upfront and honest. That meant a lot to me. I know I'm rambling but I jus wanted you to know how I feel."

When she was done all I could say was, "I'm in it for tha long haul and I'm not going to hurt you. I know what that feels like and I definitely don't like that feeling. Jazz all I ask for is communication, if there's something that's bothering you jus let me know and I'll do tha same, I promise."

I pulled into the driveway behind her car. She bolted out the car.

"You OK?"

"Yeah, I jus got to use tha bathroom real bad." I couldn't help but laugh as she rocked back and forth while unlocking the door.

"Grab tha keys Babe."

I went to get the bottle of Remy out of the fridge and then sat on the couch.

"You a'ight up there?"

"Yeah, I'm jumpin in tha shower."

"I'm gon roll me up a Dutch then."

"OK."

Between the Remy and the sour, I was feeling good. Jazz came down with a see-through nightgown on leaving nothing for the imagination.

"Damn Babe."

"What?" I just looked her up and down while licking my lips.

"See sum thing you like?"

"Yes, I do."

"So, what are you waitin for? Come get yourself sum." No need to tell you how the night ended.

CHAPTER 34

I'm Ready to Take Care of This Nigga

"I'm ready to take care of this nigga."

"Well, since I've been grabbing 20 it shouldn't be a problem to get 50 wit out causing alarm."

"You did tell him you was going all in this round."

"Let me make a call." After the third ring he picked up.

"What up?"

"You, I need 50."

"When do you need them?"

"As soon as you're ready."

"Meet me at tha spot in 1 hour."

"A'ight kool." (hung up)

"We on Bro."

"That's what I'm talkin about."

"I'm going wit you and put this on, I don't trust him." Cinco looked at Trans but instead of protesting he did as his brother advised him to.

"Do you really think he's that foolish?"

"Yes, his greed overrides his intelligence."

"You know my gut never fails me."

An hour later, we were pulling up to the warehouse and Cinco's car was already there as usual.

"Grab that duffle bag and remember on my signal." I knew he would be alone since the last few times he was.

"Hey hey my friend."

"What it do Cinco?"

"Another day another dollar."

"I heard that."

"Here you go," I said handing him the duffle bag.

"This is a mill?"

"Mill fifty."

"Here are tha 50 plus and extra 5."

Once I had the bag I said, "You know I never took it personal when you and Trans roughed me up."

"I know my Friend."

"So please don't take this personal."

Before he could ask what, Kyle had already had his pistol out. (POP-POP-POP-POP) 4 Shots to the chest dropped him where he stood. As I turned to talk to Kyle his head exploded like a melon being dropped from an eight-story building.

"What tha fuck!" I went to grab Kyle's gun and my whole back went numb.

"Aaagghh Fuck!" I saw Trans getting closer but I couldn't fuckin move.

"Cinco, Cinco," I heard him say which caused me to smile since I knew he was dead.

"Cinco get up!"

"Aaagghh Shit," he said sitting up, "what tha fuck."

"Bet you glad I told you to put that fuckin vest on now." Cinco stood up and then walked over to Pete.

"You piece of shit! Now that I did take very personal."

He whistled, then Pablo and Acis came running. He said something in Spanish in within seconds Pablo and Acis attacked Pete's body like a rag doll. He screamed for a few minutes until they had severed his head from his body. Even trans had to turn his head. Cinco commanded them to stop and they did as they were told.

"I'll call tha cleanup crew and have them take care of this." Cinco spoke more Spanish to Pablo and Acis causing them to run off.

"How in tha Hell did you get them to understand Spanish?"

"A lot of work Bro."

"I believe it."

"Let's get out of here, we got work to do."

"Well, we got sum free money."

"Yeah, but I doubt it's a mill in there."

"What ever it is, it's free for us to split."

"Right you are Lil' Bro, I definitely can't and will not complain about that."

CHAPTER 35

Sanchez Decided He'd Take Care of Strap

Sanchez decided he'd take care of Strap instead of waiting for the next man to do it. After all, he did try to take him out of the equation. Lil did he know somebody else did sum homework and was also on the hunt as well. Sanchez pulled up on Strap's block in a white dry-cleaners van and parked. He would wait all night if he had to, but he wasn't leaving until Strap was no longer amongst the living. He never knew the bombed-out black Impala had the same thoughts and was parked two cars up.

Meanwhile, Strap sat in the Safari takin down shot after shot of Patron hoping sum female worthy of taking him home would walk through the door. After another 4 shots he decided he was ready to go somewhere he really went, home. He would stop at the Dash Inn and grab a few Dutch's and snacks, then head in. His phone began to ring, when he looked at the caller ID he decided not to answer it. Not that he didn't want to but simply because he didn't feel like driving to Philly and he knew Marisol wouldn't feel like driving to Wilmington. He walked in the Dash Inn and ran into this thot named Monica.

"Damn Stranger long time no see." Strap just nodded his head up and down.

"Am I wit you tanite?"

"I got to handle some shit."

"Well, I only live around tha corner, can I catch a ride home at least?"

"How was you gon get there if you didn't see me?"

"Walk."

"Oh OK."

"Don't act like that Strap we better than that."

"Let me pay for my shit and I got you."

"Thanks, I really do appreciate it, you're a lifesaver."

"I bet," Strap thought to himself.

"You ready?"

"Waitin on you."

Monica wasn't bad looking but she was one of the biggest thots in the city. Ain't too many niggaz who can't say they slept with her. As soon as she got in the car she was on me.

"Unh, I see you still packin heat," she said rubbing my penis.

"Always Ma always."

"Well, don't you want to bust ya gun?"

I didn't respond to that instead asked, "Which way is your house?"

"Go to 10th then make a right at tha light. After that, go up 5 blocks to Rodney Street and then pull over." Once she finished with her directions she unzipped my pants and pulled my shit out.

"Oh, he not woke yet? Let me help wake him up."

Before I could even protest, not that I really wanted to, she had slid half of him into the warmness of her mouth.

"Uuumm," I said letting out a light moan.

She came up and said, "Pull up between those two cars where its dark."

This wasn't her first time using the spot, but I did as I was told.

"Let's go in my house."

"I ain't got that kind of time."

"Well, put ya back seats down."

I had to laugh to myself because she was determined to get her shit off, good thing I was in my truck.

"Turn tha ignition off."

"Nah, we good."

"OK."

"Plus, we gon to need that air conditioner." (LOL)

I pulled the seat down giving us more than enough room to take care of business. A couple came walking pass, but I knew they couldn't see us since my tint was so dark.

"Grab one of those condoms out tha glove box."

Monica had a sundress on so that made it even better. I pulled my shorts down to my ankles wasting no time sliding the condom on she jus had given me. Monica pulled her dress up exposing her pantyless clean shaven vagina. I can't front, no matter how much or big of a thot she was she never smelled and was always clean. I wasted no time busting her ass. My tint might have stopped from seeing us but all the screaming she was doing would definitely be heard if somebody walked by. I was giving it to her like it would be my last nut. Damn, I had forgotten how good Monica shot was, I felt myself about to release my load, so I started really given it to her which only made her buck even more.

"I'm a bout to cum again, that's right make this pussy cum. Oooooh I'm Cumming!" I released at the same time as she did.

"Damn, I miss this dick."

At one point, she had a nigga so fucked up I almost wifed her. (LOL) I rolled the condom off, pulled my pants up, then climbed back up front.

"Call me," she said getting out.

"You got tha same number?"

"Yup."

"A'ight, oh here," I said reaching in my pocket and handing her five $20 bills.

"Strap you know it ain't never been bout no money wit us."

"I know but after that performance."

"Shit, a bitch should be payin you, I'm tha one that got ta get eight orgasms off. Shit, a bitch been lucky to jus get one off."

"Ha! Ha! Ha!" We both laughed at that.

"Don't worry, I'll be helping you out again."

"Wheew thank you Lord."

"I'll hit you," I said pulling off.

"Damn," Sanchez said looking at his watch seeing it was a lil after 12.

"Fuck where this bitch nigga at?"

Two cars up and he was thinking the same shit. I'll wait here all night if I have to.

"Can you be my wifey."

"Hello."

"Hey Baby."

"What's good Claire?"

"Are you staying wit me tanite?"

"Yeah."

"A'ight, I won't put tha deadbolt on then."

"Kool, I should be there wit in tha next hour hopefully."

"No problem, I'll wait up for you," she said in her seductive voice.

"That's what I like to hear."

"Go grab some Dutch's too please."

"Sure will." As soon as I hung up I saw a pair of headlights approaching.

"I hope this is tha nigga cause I need to get home to my baby."

When he rode past, Sanchez slid his mask on his face, screwed his silencer on then slid out the van.

Two cars up, he was sliding his mask down his face grabbing his pistol off the passenger seat.

"Tanite you meet your maker Strap, promise you that."

Strap was on the phone with King clueless of what was going on or what he was walking into.

"Damn Nigga so you back fuckin Monica?"

A nigga forgot how good her shit was."

"Yeah, you had to detox yourself off that shit."

"I know right, if it wasn't for you and Float I would've wifed her up."

"Noooo don't do it."

"Nah, I'm good Bro."

King laughed and said, "I hope so."

Strap saw two figures approaching from his left and right side. He went to reach for his pistol then remembered he left it in his truck.

"Fuck!"

"What's up Bro?" King asked.

"I love you."

"Huh?" That's when King heard voices.

"You bitch nigga, you thought you was gonna get away with that shit. You fuck nigga you wanna throw dirt on my name now they'll throw dirt on your casket." King couldn't believe what he was hearing.

"Strap! Strap!" King yelled into the phone, "I'll see you in Hell."

"Say hello to Miguel."

Both shooters fired at the same time. SSPTT! SSPTT! SSPTT! SSPTT! SSPTT! SSPTT-SSPTT-SSPTT! Once Straps body fell both shooters stood face-to-face guns pointed at each other.

"My beef ain't wit you."

"Nor mines wit you."

They both aimed their guns toward Straps body and let off a few more rounds ending whatever chance he had left to fight. Sanchez picked up Straps phone then said he's gone before dropping the phone on his lifeless body. King was still yelling out his name as if he hadn't heard what was just said. Both shooters slid back in their vehicles and pulled off as if they hadn't just committed murder in the first degree.

CHAPTER 36

Somebody Killed Strap

Jazz ran downstairs to see why King was yelling. When she got there, she could see the tears in Kings eyes.

"Baby what's wrong?"

King looked at her, but no words would come out. She knew something terrible had happened, so she ran upstairs threw on sum sweats, sneakers, and a T-shirt.

"Come on I'll drive."

"No need to rush he's dead."

"Who Baby?"

"Strap."

My mouth fell to the floor. Once we were in the car he told me where to go.

"I need to call Float," he said pulling out his phone.

Float came on the line the same time as we were pulling up to Strap's block which was taped off.

"Yo Bro what's up?"

King could not get the words out then he heard Lee-Lee scream.

"King what's going on?" King gave Jazz the phone as they walked on the scene.

"Hello."

"Jazz what tha Hell is going on and why is my niece screaming?" Float felt it in the pit of his stomach that something bad happened.

"Excuse me Sir I need you to stay back."

"Get off of me that's my brother!"

The detective gave the cop a head nod to let me and Jazz by. I walked right up and kneeled down beside Strap's body.

"I must warn you, it's horrible," the detective said.

As soon as I pulled the sheet back I almost lost my stomach. Strap's face was totally disfigured, he would definitely have a closed casket. At that moment, I didn't care, I picked his lifeless body up and held it to mines.

"Nooooo!"

As soon as Float heard King scream he knew the worse had happen his brother from another was gone. When Jazz heard King scream out it broke her, then seconds later she heard Float do the same thing.

"Hello-hello." It was Mayla on the line.

"Hey Mayla."

"Jazz what is going on?"

"Sum body killed Strap."

"Oh My God! Are you serious? Never mind, dumb question, we're on our way down."

"A'ight," I said hanging up, so I could be by King's side.

The coroner was try'n to get King to release Strap's body but what he wouldn't. The detective understood so he asked the medical examiner to give him some time. Lee-Lee jus kept calling for her daddy. My heart was hurting for them. In the months that I had been with King I knew how Strap felt about Lee-Lee and vice versa. Even though Lee-Lee mom Keri and Strap were not together they still had a strong bond and relationship. Keri held her daughter as they both cried. I heard somebody yell get the Fuck off of me and I need to see my brothers.

At that point, I knew Float had arrived. The same detective nodded to let him pass. By now, Kings clothes were soaked in Straps' blood but he refused to let him go. Float dropped to his knees grabbing both King and Strap. When Lee-Lee saw her other uncle she really lost it.

After few more minutes, the detective had to let them know they had to let the medical examiner do his job. To all of our surprise, both Float and King laid his body back down gently and got up. Both King as well as Float had a look in their eyes and the detective saw it also.

"Listen fellas, I know that you are hurt but please do not take matters into your own hands let the WPD handle this."

"We are," Float said but the detective did not believe them.

Besides Lee-Lee and Keri we are the only family he has, Float said to no one in particular. They both walked over to where Keri and Lee-Lee stood. Seeing the pain in Lee-Lee eyes caused both of them to cry.

Float said, "He will be remembered as long as I have breath in my body, I promise."

"Keri," King said barely audible.

"Yes."

"Can you handle all of tha arrangements for his funeral? Don't worry about the cost."

"Yeah, he's going out in style."

"I will handle it," she said with tears in her eyes, "I didn't even get to tell him that I'm pregnant," she said then cried even harder.

They all looked at her even Lee-Lee.

"Pregnant?" Lee-Lee asked.

"Yes 14 weeks, I jus found out yesterday."

Before we could ask she said, "Yes it's Straps baby."

"Damn, I knew y'all was still messing around," Float said.

That caused Keri to smile a lil bit.

"I guess this is good news on a sad night."

Even though Lee-Lee was only 7 she clearly understood what was goin on. Mayla and Jazz came over to show their support. Keri met Jazz, but this was her first introduction to Mayla.

"I know you don't know us like that, but we are here if you need us."

"Yeah, Keri even if it's jus an ear to listen or shoulder to lean on."

"Thanks y'all, I really appreciate it, I really do."

"No problem, Strap was family."

It felt good for King and Float to hear both their ladies extend their hands and say that.

"His last words to me was I love you."

"Huh."

"I was on tha phone wit him when it went down." They all looked at King who was crying.

"We were talking then all of a sudden he yelled Fuck…" King stopped and put his head down. Everybody waited for him to finish.

"He yelled Fuck! I asked him what was wrong. That's when he said I love you. He knew it was his end."

King looked at Float, "Bro I heard two people talkin."

"Did you hear what they said or recognize tha voices?"

"I didn't recognize tha voices, but I heard one say or ask Strap did he think he was going to get away wit that shit. Then tha other one said something about him throwing dirt on his name and now dirt will be thrown on his casket." Hearing this really pissed Float off.

"Keri take Lee-Lee home, we'll be by in tha morning."

"OK."

"We love you Baby girl."

"I love y'all too."

CHAPTER 37

Who Killed Strap?

"Yo, I know you heard by now what happened to your boy."

"Who is my boy Dae-Dae?"

"Strap."

"Nah, I didn't hear."

"Oh nah, he got killed last night."

"I know."

"What? I thought you said..." Dae-Dae stopped mid-sentence understanding exactly what it was Sanchez was saying.

"From what they sayin it was two people."

Sanchez just shrugged his shoulders. Spanish Jose pulled up bumpin that classic "If I Die Tonight."

"Yo."

"What it do Sanchez?"

"Same shit."

"Jus wanted to say good look on tha information tha other day."

"UAlready."

"Heard oh boy checked out last night."

"Yeah, that's what tha word is."

"Niggaz can't think they can get away wit shit."

"Guess they'll be throwing dirt on his casket."

It was at that moment they both knew they were the reason Strap was no longer breathing without saying nothing else they dapped each other and went their separate ways.

"You think King and Float gon be on some dumb shit?"

"They don't know who did it."

"True."

"Even if they did they don't want what I'm giving out facts."

"I Got Blood on My Money and I Still Spend it."

"What you know bout that Cannon?"

"Come on, you know I fuck wit Future hard body."

"He got tha game in a choke hold right now."

"He got a concert comin up at Wells Fargo next month."

"Grab me two tickets when you get yours."

"Me too."

"I got y'all, I'll tell Tessa cause she gon be tha one ordering them."

"We got a fresh shipment comin today."

"That's what's up cause all my folks comin thru today."

"Shit mines too."

"Well, you know there's a drought comin guess niggaz heard."

"Damn, how long that shit gon be tha last time it was a drought that shit lasted damn near three months."

"Bro, I don't know, but what I do know is it won't affect us this time."

"Oh word?"

"Yup, Tayo assured me, said he's never affected by it, doesn't even know what no drought is."

"Well, in that case I can't wait for it. Ha! Ha! Ha!"

"Drought means prices go up though."

"Yeah, for our folks, but not us."

"Damn Tayo really is tha Fuckin plug."

"Yeah, cause most people would take clear advantage of that and sky rocket tha number."

"We jus gon jump tha number two points."

"Nah Bro, I say three, you know in tha drought when niggaz get they hands on shit they charge up to 32-33k a brick so 28k is nothing but love not to mention, niggaz going to step, no correction stomp all on it."

"Damn you right, I ain't even consider that, we might go 29-30k jus because of that."

"I'm telling you niggaz ain't gon to care cause they gon to turn one into two all day."

"True that."

A few days later, the drought was definitely on. When I pulled up to Tessa's Tayo was already there. I had to laugh cause I'm always early and he still beats me there.

"Hey Baby," Tessa said as soon as I walked in the door.

"Hey Babe."

"Cannon."

"Tayo."

"Did I not tell you a drought was comin?"

"Yeah, you definitely did."

"No worries, it will not affect us negatively anyway."

"I know, I'll be runnin thru a lot now."

"You do that anyway."

"Yeah, but I'm damn near out already."

"Oh yeah?"

"Yeah, my folks been comin so much and they comin for their folks I'm not dealing wit no new people."

"That is good you make them go through your people."

"Are you charging 32-34k?"

"Nah, I'm jus charging them 30k."

Tayo smiled, "Never tha greedy one I see."

"Nope and to be honest, I only charge that cause I know they steppin on it so they still winning."

"Right you are."

"Cannon I must admit you have far exceeded my expectations." This causes both Cannon and Tessa to smile.

"What are you smiling for Tess?"

"I'm happy that my baby is doin his thing."

"As you should be."

"Tha last time you tried to look out for a friend it cost him dearly."

Tessa's smile quickly faded as she thought back on how Mike tried to play her dad and had paid with his life.

"Some people are jus so small-minded they can't see tha bigger picture."

"This is true, that's why I had my doubts at first wit Cannon."

Sum times love will blind you and have you doing things that you wouldn't normally do."

"Tayo if a man or woman isn't use to having money or anything for that matter then when they get it you instantly see tha change."

"True."

"Wit me, I've always got and had money since I stepped off tha porch so gettin wit you and seeing all tha money I see now it didn't change me, it only made me appreciate it that much more cause at any moment it can be gon."

"You are very smart."

"I know that a lot of good people get caught up wit having so much work that they deal wit any and ery body to get rid of it which ultimately leads to their demise." Tayo shook his head knowing I was speaking facts.

"Me, yeah, I would love to dump 200 kilos a week, but not at tha cost of going to jail so I'm more than OK dumping that amount every two weeks." Tessa facial expressions said Damn Baby. (LOL)

"I'm not greedy nor selfish, I learned early you gotta make sure tha ones you truly Fuck wit too. Jealousy breeds envy and envy breeds hate." After hearing all this Tayo gained a new-found respect for Cannon.

"I see Sanchez took care of that problem we talked about over lunch." My facial expression must have showed what I was thinking.

"You don't remember do you?"

"Honestly no."

"I'm speaking of that problem wit tha voice he didn't recognize."

"Oh wow, I didn't know that, we have not had a chance to talk on that it's been all bizness."

"I did hear that he was no longer among tha living though." Tessa was try'n to figure out who they were talking about.

"Well, I have a few things to handle so let me know when you are ready."

"We can handle that when you are finished taking care of your bizness, I'm in no rush. Besides it's not like the money is goin anywhere."

Tayo smiled and said, "I will call you when ery thing is in motion."

"Kool, no problem." Tayo hugged Tessa then left.

"Baby my dad is really fond of you."

"That's a good thing isn't it? I would hate to end up like Mike."

"That would never happen, y'all cut from to totally different cloths."

"Wit out a doubt, I should've took you from him."

"Excuse me?"

"You heard me."

"What makes you think I would have jump ship?"

"Tessa, I understand that you were in love, but I also know you weren't happy."

"What makes you say that?"

"Do you see how you always smile now and have that glow about you? You didn't have that before."

"So, you're sayin you make me happy?"

"Wouldn't you?"

"No argument there."

"My question is why stay wit sum one who doesn't make you happy?"

"You said it; I was in love."

"Then why tell Tayo what he was doing or try'n to do?"

"Simple my loyalty is to my father."

"Would you do tha same if it were me?"

"Of course, I would."

"I would hope so. I don't have to worry about that wit you though."

"Why not?"

"You're not greedy."

"Cannon you know I love you, don't you?"

"Yes, I do."

"Good, as long as you know that."

"I love you also."

"Do you?" I looked at her, "I'm jus playing, I know you do."

"As long as you know it. Oh, before I forget, when you order those tickets for Future order four more."

"Damn so 10 altogether?"

"I don't know, but Dae-Dae and Sanchez both want two."

"Well, Taylor and Claire asked me to order them sum."

"Well, jus get 6 then. Make sure they're floor seats."

"Damn, and to think I was gon to get those nosebleed seats."

"Jus makin sure Smartass."

"Jus Like Brothers treat him jus like a brother."

"What up Bro?"

"About time to send Tessa to tha beauty salon while prices are low."

"Yeah, she's goin after she finish runnin around."

"Oh OK, I need to rap wit you though where you at?"

"Leavin Jersey."

"Kool, hit me when you get back."

"A'ight I should be back in bout a ½, you could jus meet me outside." (code for the block)

"Kool."

I was already outside when Sanchez pulled up. We greeted each other then I got straight to bizness.

"Yo Nigga, why I had to find out through Tayo you slumped Strap?"

"Damn how tha Fuck that nigga be knowing so fucking much?"

"I don't know."

"He gave me tha run down on what took place."

"What tha Fuck were tha chances you two niggaz set out on tha same mission that night?"

"Same Shit I thought."

"Funny how shit works out sum times."

"Hey Bro, it was his time."

"I guess so, but speaking of Spanish Jose, he stepped to me tha other day."

"What you mean step to you?"

"Nah, Nah, on sum money Shit."

"Oh, OK Claire told me she told Tessa to order us sum tickets."

"I know she told me when I told her."

"Well, I'm bout to go handle that now."

"Hit me when you do."

CHAPTER 38

Strap's Funeral

Strap's funeral was pretty packed, mostly everybody had on white instead of the traditional black that was always worn at funerals. Keri and Lee-Lee were sitting in the front row along with me, Float, Mayla, and Jazz. Would've never thought I would see Strap on the front of so many T-shirts. I hadn't been able to eat or sleep since his murder. I had no way of finding out who had done this and that's what hurt me the most. Since It was a closed casket a big picture of Strap set on an easel above his casket. You could hear the crying throughout the church. I don't think there was a dry eye in the place. I know Strap did his bullshit, but let's be honest who doesn't. Lee-Lee got up to read her poem, me and Float decided to take her to the podium since Keri was unable to do it. She opened up her paper and started reading, it was more of a letter than a poem.

Dad,

I know that you're in Heaven looking down on us wishing you could still be here. I'm missing you so much and so is Mommy, Uncle King and Uncle Float. Hey, guess what you're having another baby, but don't worry he's going to look jus like you. Why did you leave me Daddy, why?

She couldn't finish, she broke down and seeing her so emotional broke me down. I picked her up and she melted in my arms.

"I got you Baby it's gon be OK."

The pallbearers carried his casket to the hearse. Once the Rev said his final prayer Strap was lowered into what would be his final resting spot.

After everybody else left I decided to stay. I told Jazz to get the car and come back to get me.

"Well Bro, I'm so mad right now I can't even think straight. Your death has me reevaluating this whole life I'm living right now. At any moment, it could be my time. So, I've been asking myself is it even worth it anymore? Maybe I should jus invest the money I have, go all in on black." I saw Jazz pull up, but I didn't move not that I didn't want to, but my feet wouldn't let me.

"Baby you a'ight?"

"I will be."

"It takes time."

"I know, I'm ready let's go."

As soon as we got in the car I put on my Biggie Life After Death CD and played Missing You. *"Oooohh I'm Missing You Tell Me Why This Hurts."* I must have listened to that song a thousand times.

"Do you want to go home or to tha repass?"

Before I could respond she said, "Lee-Lee was lookin and askin for you."

"Well, that answers your question. I'll be in, I need to smoke first."

I put my shades back on as I lit my blunt and turned the volume back up on my radio. By the time I finished my Dutch I was high as shit. I saw Lee-Lee standing in the doorway of the hall waving me in.

"I thought you weren't coming," she said jumping in my arms.

"You good Bro?"

"Yeah, jus had to talk to bro."

"I know you feeling sum type of way since you was on tha phone wit him."

"Bro you have no ideal, this is tearing me up, I haven't eaten or slept. Ery time I close my eyes I jus picture him getting his face blown off."

I definitely felt King's pain, it was like a part of me had been destroyed. I looked at King and could tell he wanted to say something.

"What's on ya mind Bro?"

"I'm thinkin about leaving tha game alone." Out of all things that was definitely not what I expected to hear.

"Leaving tha game alone? Are you sure?"

"Truthfully, I don't know, but this pain I'm feeling is worse than what I felt when I found out that Banita was carrying another man's baby."

I remember how that tore him up since he was so excited about finally becoming a father. Only to catch her cheating, then admitting the baby was not his.

"(Ouch) Well, if that's what you want to do then do it, but I'm in this til six carry me or 12 judge me."

"Float was right, so over tha next few days I definitely have a lot to think about."

"King do you think Cannon or Sanchez had anything to do wit this?"

"I had considered that, but I doubt it, they would've handled that tha day tha shit went down on their block."

"Yeah, you probably right. Don't rush into any decisions that you might regret jus let me know and I know tha drought is on. So, what is tha damage?"

"Not sure, but I think 32k."

"That ain't bad, I know this is not tha time nor place, but I need to get my hands on a few."

"What's a few Bro?"

"At least 5."

"I'll make a call to Gotti."

"Thanks," I said giving him a brotherly hug.

CHAPTER 39

Future is in the Building

"Damn, I'm glad I got us reserved parking."

"I know, Future brought them out tanite." We all pulled in the reserved parking lot then made our way to the building.

"I need to hit this bar up before I go to my seat."

"We all need a drink."

"These lines long as Fuck."

"Who you telling."

"Imma get me two double shot so I ain't got to come back and deal wit this shit. Let me see if I can buy sum body's drink ta cut this line."

By the time we made it to our seats Future was already performing Stick Talk. We wasted no time lighting up our Dutch's. Future ran through his rolodex of hits nonstop. When it was over he told everybody to meet him at Vanity Grand for his after party.

"Damn, let me call to get us a booth." We pulled up to Vanity and it was J-peed.

"What up Homie?"

"We felt up."

"Tony saved us three spots."

"They ain't tell me nothing."

"Hold up, let me call him up."

I made the call and Tony came out. We pulled into the spots he saved for us.

"My fault main Man."

"It ain't bout nuffin you jus doin ya job." Tony took us through the side door.

"How you doin Cannon?"

"You know Tony bout to turn up."

"I feel you."

"Imma need 6 bottles, Ciroc, Remy, 2 Henny's, and 2 Bombay's."

"A'ight."

"We also need 60k worth of ones."

"Oh, you ain't bullshit'n tanite."

"I never bullshit Tony."

He showed us to our booth then said the bottles and ones will be right up. All eyes were on us because our jewels lit up the whole club. It was some nigggaz in the next booth who were trying a little too hard to impress the crowd if you ask me.

I could hear one of the strippers say, "Throw that Shit stop holding on to it."

I had to laugh which caused him to say, "Baby girl this shit ain't bout nothing."

"Awwee Shit! Tha party bout ta get started," the DJ said when he noticed the 6 bottles and 3 trays of ones.

Most of the strippers that were in their booths.

Lil over 2 hours…

"Babe you want some of these?" I asked Tessa.

"Sure, why not."

"Fuck up Sum Comma's a Hundred Thousand and a Hundred Thousand Fuck up Sum Comma's Tanite."

"We definitely came to Fuck up sum commas tanite."

I handed Tessa one of the bags, so she could do her. One of the strippers asked Dae-Dae if we rapped or played ball.

"Nah, we own our own bizness." I couldn't help but laugh when he said that.

"Future is in tha building," the DJ announced which made whatever strippers we didn't have flock to him.

We continued to make it rain ones til we were all ready to go. We ended up fuckin up about 120k easy. Tony let us know he appreciated our bizness then said that from now on we could get a booth for the low since we always dropped at least 30k when we came through. Me and Tessa decided to hit the Waffle House in Maryland before we went home.

CHAPTER 40

The Drought Was Still On

It had been a few days since the funeral I was still at it. Float just called to say he'd be down for 5. I can't even believe the drought was still on and the only one who had work was Cannon and his squad. He had one Hell of a plug to still have Grade A work and never running out. I wanted to wave the white flag and holla at him, but my pride wouldn't let me do it. I pulled out my phone and called Gotti.

"Yo."

"What up folk?"

"Same shit."

"Imma need you in bout an hour if you around."

"I'll be around."

"Kool, you got 10 on deck?"

"Yup."

"A'ight, hit you in an hour."

"No doubt."

One hour later, I was headed back to the stash house after meeting Gotti. I saw the red and blue lights flashing behind me.

"What the Fuck? Damn," I said looking at the duffle bag wit10 bricks in it.

"License, registration, and insurance please." I handed him my paperwork.

"Do you know why I stopped you?"

"No."

"Your left tail light is out."

"Oh OK, I didn't know."

"I'll be right back."

"Damn," I said as another car pulled up. I already had my mind made up that I was takin 'em if they ask me to step out.

"Here you go," he said handing me back my paperwork.

"Thanks."

"I'm gon let you slide wit a warning, get that fixed A.S.A.P."

"I'm gon to take care of that right now."

"A'ight, have a nice day."

"You do tha same officer."

"Damn that was close King."

"Damn Nigga, what you had too rough that nigga up?"

"Nah, I got swung by them boys."

"For what?"

"My tail light is out."

"Better get that fixed."

"Bout to head to Tom's now. Thought a nigga was gon to have to run 'em. Ha! ha! Ha!"

"Didn't you have it hid?"

"Nah."

"You better stop playing wit them people."

"You ain't got to tell me Bro."

"A'ight, I'm bout ta head back up be safe and get that light taken care of."

"You be safe too Bro."

UAlready."

"Isn't She Lovely Isn't She Wonderful."

"Hey there Beautiful."

"Hey Baby."

"You a'ight."

"Yeah, I'm jus checkin on you."

"Thanks."

"Did you eat today?"

"Nah, I'm not hungry."

"Baby you need to eat sum thing, you can't keep not eating."

"I know, but I haven't had much of an appetite. Are you busy now?"

"Nah, jus got my tail light fixed."

"Come by my office, I got a snack for you."

"Snack? What kind of snack?"

"Come see and don't be long I'll be there in a few minutes." I was literally there in a few minutes since I was only a couple blocks away.

"Hey Kandis, how are you doin?"

"I'm doin fine, how about you?"

"I'm hanging in there."

"That's good, go head back she's waiting for you." (Knock-Knock)

"Come in."

"Hey Babe."

"Hey you."

"Damn no hug no kiss?"

"Always for you," I said holding my arms out for a hug.

She walked into them and planted a big soft kiss on my lips. I grabbed a handful of ass and got an instant erection. We hadn't had sex since Strap was killed it was my shit. She went to lock the door.

"You do know Kandis is out there?" As if on cue the intercom buzzed.

"Yes Kandice."

"I'm bout to go get lunch, you want sum thing?"

"Where you going?"

"Probably get sum take out from T.G.I. Friday."

"Well, get me that Jack Daniel's steak and shrimp."

"Does hubby want sum thing?" I looked at King who nodded his head no.

"No."

"Ok, it's my treat since you treated last time."

"You sure?"

"Yeah, I got it."

"Kool, lock ya door on ya way out."

"OK, I didn't have any appointments this afternoon anyway." As soon as I heard the door shut I was all on King.

"Come on Baby give me sum a bitch is horny as Fuck."

"Ha! Ha! Ha! I'm sorry bout that."

"It's fine, trust me I understand."

Since Jazz had on a dress it made my job a lot easier. When I pulled her dress up I was surprised that she didn't have any panties on.

"What? They in my purse, I took them off when you said you will be here in a few minutes."

I didn't even respond, I just took my hand and gently petted her kitty kat. "Ooohh" was the sound that escaped her mouth. Jazz reached for my belt and with one quick motion she unbuckled my belt while pulling my shorts down. I took my penis and rubbed the head against her swollen clit.

"MMM AAAGGHH that feels so good Baby."

"Does it?"

"Yeeees." I lifted her up then slowly slid her down on my penis.

"Aaaah," she said softly in my ear.

A few soft slow strokes and Jazz was losing her mind.

"OH MY GOD Baby right there! Keep hittin that spot please," she begged me.

Who was I to deny her of what she wanted. After a few more strokes like that she was releasing her load all over me, but I didn't stop and before long she was Cumming again. It seemed as if I had found that magic cum button (LOL) because she could not stop Cuming. I was surprised that after 30 minutes I was still standing there holding her as she continued to have orgasm after orgasm. I heard the front door open, so I put her down.

"Why did you stop?"

"Kandice jus came in."

"So," she said clearly mad. The intercom buzzed.

"Yes."

"I'm back."

"Could you bring it to me please?" King unlocked the door.

"I thought you got lost."

"Nah, I should've called it in first."

"Thank you."

"No problem."

As soon as she was out the door Jazz locked it and pointed to the couch.

When I didn't move she said, "Don't make me snap."

"Babe we can finish tanite."

"No, we're gonna finish now and I'll get around 2 tanite."

"Damn you had about 4 orgasms."

"7, but who's counting? Now come on, I need to get this other one out since you stopped right when I was about to."

When I still made no attempt to move she said, "OK have it your way."

She lifted her dress up and walked over to me. Jazz pulled my pants back down then straddled me.

"Oooohh Yeees!"

I put my finger up to her lips then said, "Sssshh."

"OK, OK, Mmm," she said as she adjusted herself so that I could hit that magical spot once again.

As soon as I did... "Baaaby I'm Cuming again." This went on for another 30 minutes until Kandice buzzed the intercom.

"Uughh, yes Kandice."

"Mrs. Tibett is here to see you."

"A'ight, send her back. Shit I forgot about her. I'll see you tanite and you owe me 10 nuts."

"12, but again who's counting?"

I opened the door jus as she was about to knock. Before I walked out Jazz smiled, blew me a kiss and said thanks Babe.

"You're very welcome, see you later."

"Love you."

"Love you more."

"All young love," she said as she entered the office.

CHAPTER 41

Street Dreamz

Winter had crept back up and believe it or not we were still the only ones with work.

"Damn Bro, it's been 3½ months and still ain't no work around."

"You complaining?"

"Hell nah, we getting all tha money."

"Oh OK, thought you was (LOL) at this rate tha way my stash setup after one more flip I will accomplish my goal I set when I first started in tha game."

"What's that?"

"A million dollars."

"Damn Dae-Dae you ain't been playing."

"Jus think niggaz told me that wasn't nothing but a street dream."

"Oh yeah, one that you made reality."

"Not counting ya money, but I know that ain't shit to you and Cannon.

"No comment." (LOL)

"Speaking of, I ain't been seeing bro like that, is he bout to fall back from tha game?"

"Truthfully, ever since Tessa found out she was pregnant he's been spending all his time wit her."

"I can respect that."

"My dad is so happy, he's been wanting for me or Claire to make him a grandpa for so long."

"I know you told me."

"I told him I'm about to chill until you have tha baby."

"Baby I still got 5½ months."

"OK and I have more than enough money, shit I can quit if I want to."

"I wasn't saying it like that."

"Besides he knows Sanchez is more than capable of runnin tha ship."

"I'm pretty sure he is."

"Babe if you don't want me to spend more time and cater to you then that's fine."

"Now did I say that?"

"I'm jus sayin."

"Boy you gon make me punch on you."

"Ha! Ha! Ha!"

"Keep laughing if you want."

"Babe I'll be back I gotta go handle sum thing."

"Where you going?"

"Ta my aunts."

"Be careful I don't trust your cousin."

45 minutes later, I pulled up to my aunt's house.

"What up Deandre?"

"Money."

"I heard that."

"You got 100, right?"

"Yeah, I told you tha ticket is 30K."

"I know, it's all there," he said pointing at the duffle bag on the floor.

I bent down to grab it, but when I stood back up I was staring down the nose of a 45.

"What's tha deal Cuz?"

"Nigga you know what it is don't turn this into no homicide."

"Fuck this about?"

"You eatin so I'm sure this hundred light to you." I was wondering if I could grab my nina fast enough.

"Cuz don't do it." As soon as I tried all I heard was boom and saw a bright flash.

"Cannon, Cannon, Cannon." I jumped up.

"Baby go get yourself ready."

I got out of bed face wet from sweating. When I got to the bathroom I rinsed my face with cold water and looked in the mirror.

"Damn that was one Hell of a dream. Yeah, definitely ain't built for tha streets that dream was to real. I'll stick to my 9 to 5 at tha bank."

After getting dressed I jumped in my S550, pushed play on my CD player, then headed to work listening to *"Street Dreams are Made Off these Streets Niggaz Pushing Beamers and 300 E's a Drug Dealers Destiny is Reaching tha Keys Ery Body is Looking for Sum Thing."*

I looked in my rearview and thought, *"STREET DREAMZ ERY THING AIN'T WHAT IT SEEMS..."*

ABOUT THE AUTHOR

My name is Jerz Toston, I reside in Wilmington, Delaware. First, thanks to my fans for your continued support. This is my 3rd book titled Street Dreamz. My other 2 books, Betrayal & Deceit and Who Can U Trust are available now on all on-line bookstores. Or you can call my publisher directly at 877.782.5550 and have it shipped to your door.

Writing books is my passion and I'll continue to give you page turners. Just call me ya Fav Author.

www.ingramcontent.com/pod-product-compliance
Lightning Source LLC
Chambersburg PA
CBHW071521110726
47908CB00003B/913